"If my s〔...〕o cause problems for you...

"I don't care what anyone says about me." Besides, her family had been the topic of gossip for years in Paradise. Alonso would give them something new to chat about.

Seconds ticked by, then Alonso reached across the seat and brushed a strand of loose hair from her face. She didn't want the night to end. Didn't want to leave his side.

"Alonso?"

"What?"

"Do you ever get lonely?" Until she'd sat across the table from him at the restaurant, Hannah hadn't consciously acknowledged the depth of her loneliness.

"Yes." His quiet answer made her heart pound.

This is crazy. You hardly know the man.

She couldn't argue with the voice in her head but the strength to resist a night in Alonso's arms had fled the instant he'd pulled her close on the dance floor. "I don't want to be alone tonight," she whispered.

He leaned across the seat and slid his hand around the back of her neck. "I don't want to be alone, either."

And then he kissed her.

Dear Reader,

The world can be a scary, ugly place. Many of us have given up, thrown in the towel or lost hope at one time or another. It's usually during those dark days when someone comes into our lives and shows us that not all is lost.

In *The Surgeon's Christmas Baby*, no one is more world-weary than Alonso Marquez. As a trauma surgeon he's seen far too much death and destruction to hold any faith in humanity. That is until he meets Hannah Buck. Hannah shows Alonso that love is the key to unlocking the beauty and goodness which still exists in the world. When Hannah becomes pregnant by accident, Alonso is terrified of bringing a child into a world where bad always wins over good. It's only through Hannah's love that Alonso finds the courage to leave the darkness behind and reach for a life filled with love and joy that only a family can bring.

I hope you enjoy Alonso and Hannah's journey to their very own happy-ever-after. If you missed the first story in the Cowboys of the Rio Grande series, *The Cowboy's Redemption* (June 2015) is still available through your favorite online retailers.

You can find out more about me and my books at marinthomas.com. I love to connect with my readers and invite you to follow me on Facebook at facebook.com/AuthorMarinThomas and Twitter at twitter.com/MarinThomas.

Happy reading!

Marin

THE SURGEON'S CHRISTMAS BABY

—

Marin Thomas

HARLEQUIN® AMERICAN ROMANCE®

Recycling programs
for this product may
not exist in your area.

ISBN-13: 978-0-373-75593-6

The Surgeon's Christmas Baby

Copyright © 2015 by Brenda Smith-Beagley

Printed in U.S.A.

Marin Thomas grew up in the Midwest, then attended college at the U of A in Tucson, Arizona, where she earned a BA in radio-TV and played basketball for the Lady Wildcats. Following graduation she married her college sweetheart in the historic Little Chapel of the West in Las Vegas, Nevada. Recently empty nesters, Marin and her husband now live in Texas, where cattle is king, cowboys are plentiful and pickups rule the road. Visit her on the web at marinthomas.com.

Books by Marin Thomas

Harlequin American Romance

The Cash Brothers

The Cowboy Next Door
Twins Under the Christmas Tree
Her Secret Cowboy
The Cowboy's Destiny
True Blue Cowboy
A Cowboy of Her Own

Rodeo Rebels

Rodeo Daddy
The Bull Rider's Secret
A Rodeo Man's Promise
Arizona Cowboy
A Cowboy's Duty
No Ordinary Cowboy

Cowboys of the Rio Grande

A Cowboy's Redemption

Visit the Author Profile page
at Harlequin.com for more titles.

To my great-niece Adley Faith:
You are braver than you believe,
stronger than you seem and
smarter than you think.
Follow your dreams and never look back.

Chapter One

"Quit lookin' at me like that."

Darn Luke's ornery hide. Hannah Buck squeezed the steering wheel, wishing it was her half brother's neck.

Yesterday after lunch Luke had left the ranch to attend a Halloween party with friends. He'd promised to be home by dark, but ten o'clock had come and gone and Hannah had paced the kitchen floor, imagining him lying dead in a ditch somewhere—just as she'd found their father two years ago.

"You could have texted me that you were staying the night at Connor's."

"I left my cell phone at home."

On purpose. When their father died, the court had appointed Hannah Luke's legal guardian—a job she'd gladly accepted. But she hadn't counted on her then fourteen-year-old brother embarking on a mission to make her life miserable.

The recent skipping school, drinking and smoking pot had to stop. She'd attributed Luke's rebellion to grief and in the beginning hadn't demanded too much of him. Even his teachers had gone easy on him. But two years had passed since their father's death and Luke's behavior was getting out of hand. If he didn't settle down and quit running wild, he'd end up in jail, and then she wouldn't be able to save his butt.

"I can't do this anymore, Luke."

"Do what?"

That he had to ask showed how little he cared about the responsibility resting on her shoulders. "I can't take care of the ranch and chase after you. It's time for you to grow up."

"Jeez…not another lecture." He sprawled across the backseat. "You didn't have to come get me. I could have driven home."

If Connor's mother hadn't informed Hannah that she and her husband were leaving town, Luke would have remained at his friend's the entire day and skipped out on doing his chores. She glanced in the rearview mirror. Her brother had turned sixteen five months ago, but his smooth skin and pudgy cheeks reminded her of the little boy who'd followed her everywhere on the ranch. Hannah had been the only one who'd paid attention to him when their father was lost in the bottle or Luke's mother, Ruth, left on one of her weekend getaways.

Hannah and Luke had grown even closer after Ruth died in a car accident right before Luke's tenth birthday. She recalled the afternoon her father broke the news to them—Luke hadn't shed a tear. Instead, he'd asked Hannah to play a video game with him. She hadn't been surprised that her brother had turned to her, since Ruth had assigned all the mothering duties to ten-year-old Hannah when she'd brought Luke home from the hospital.

To be honest, she hadn't been distraught over Ruth's death, either. It was hard to shed a tear for the woman who'd caused her parents' divorce. Hannah hadn't heard from her mother—not even a birthday card—since the day she'd walked out on her family. Hannah wished she could blame Ruth for her mother abandoning her but that wouldn't be fair. The sad truth was that all the adults in her and Luke's life had let them down.

After their father's funeral Hannah had discovered how badly he'd mismanaged the ranch. Instead of spending time with Luke, she'd spent days poring over financial records with an accountant at the bank. He'd set up a payment plan with her creditors and she'd been forced to let their ranch hand go. Keeping the business from going under had fallen on her shoulders, but she'd accepted the responsibility, hoping Luke would help out, but like a typical teenager all he cared about was hanging with his friends.

"How am I supposed to get my car?" he asked.

"We'll pick it up tomorrow." As far as Hannah was concerned, *her* old Civic could sit on the Henderson property a good long while. Without wheels Luke would be stuck at home and maybe out of sheer boredom he'd do his chores. "How much did you and Connor drink last night?"

"Enough."

She still hadn't broken the news to her brother that she'd been asked to keep him away from Connor. Mrs. Henderson believed Luke was a bad influence on her son. The apple didn't fall far from the tree.

She couldn't remember a time her father hadn't reached for a beer when he walked into the house—morning, noon or night. He'd kept his drinking under control until Ruth died. Hannah wasn't sure if her father's depression had been caused by Ruth's death or learning the *girlfriend* in the car with her at the time of the accident had been a man named Stan Smith.

"You can't keep this up, Luke." When he remained silent, she said, "You know Dad was an alcoholic. You carry the gene." If worrying about her brother's drinking wasn't enough stress, yesterday afternoon she'd discovered an acre of fence had been torn down and several of their bison had wandered onto the neighbor's property. Roger Markham hadn't been pleased when he'd had to send his ranch hands to round up her livestock.

She'd reported the vandalism to Sheriff Miller, who'd attributed it to a Halloween prank by local kids. He'd promised to notify his deputies to be on the lookout for any troublemakers in the Paradise area. Then he'd suggested that until they caught the culprits, Hannah should take Luke with her when she checked the herd—as if that was going to happen.

"Not that you care, but some jerk trampled a section of fence and the bison wandered onto the Los Pinos Ranch." Hannah had insurance to cover the cost of repairing the fence, but the deductible was a thousand dollars. There went her Christmas fund.

"Who gives a crap about those stupid animals?" The truck hit a bump and he groaned. "Watch your driving."

She was tempted to slam on the brakes, put the truck into Reverse and drive back and forth over the pothole until Luke puked. "When we get home, I need you to load the hay bales onto the flatbed."

"I'm too tired."

If she gripped the wheel any tighter, she'd rip it from the steering column. Hannah had planned to go to college after she'd graduated from high school, but then Ruth had died and her father had sunk into a deep depression and she'd ended up staying put. Even so, she'd never regret spending those last few years with her father. Helping him run the ranch had given her a deeper appreciation for rural life, and now she couldn't imagine doing anything else. Eventually she was confident Luke's view of the ranch would change, too, and he'd see the value of his inheritance. Right now, she had to worry about weathering this latest storm with him.

"You know that Dad probably wouldn't have died that night if he hadn't been—"

"Drinking. I know."

Hannah didn't like bringing up their father's death, but she never wanted Luke to forget. He needed the reminder, especially now when he was experimenting with alcohol and drugs. She didn't want him to make stupid decisions that would put his life in danger—like going for a horseback ride after drinking a twelve-pack of beer.

Joe Buck hadn't ridden far when he'd lost his balance and had fallen off Buster, cracking his head open. By the time Hannah had noticed the horse wandering aimlessly in the ranch yard, it had been too late. She'd found her father's lifeless body in a ravine behind the house, his hand clutching a beer can.

"You can take a nap after you load the hay," she said. The herd should have been fed this morning, but she'd wasted the past two hours fetching Luke.

"You're not my mom. You can't tell me what to do."

The jab hurt. She'd been more of a mother to Luke than Ruth ever had. Hannah had been the one to make her brother's breakfast before school. Not Ruth. Hannah had done the family's laundry and made sure Luke's Little League uniform had been ready to wear on Saturday morning. Not Ruth. And when Luke had taken Melissa Walter to the school dance this past spring, Hannah had been the one to purchase a box of condoms and give Luke a safe sex lecture. Not Ruth.

"You've been running wild since Dad died and it's got to stop. If you'd help out more, we could expand the herd." *And I could keep an eye on you.* The thought of something terrible happening to Luke terrified Hannah. They might be at odds right now but he was all the family she had left, and she loved her brother.

"Bison suck."

"They're keeping a roof over our heads and food on the table."

"Connor said his father thinks Dad was stupid to buy bison instead of cattle."

Hannah was well aware that their neighbors believed raising bison for specialty meat markets was a waste of good land. "I don't care what Mr. Henderson thinks."

"School's dumb. I wanna drop out."

It took a moment for Hannah's mind to switch gears. "What do you mean you want to quit school?" At least from six-thirty in the morning until three-thirty in the afternoon, Monday through Friday she knew where her brother was.

"I'm not learning anything."

"You're staying in school, Luke."

"Just 'cause you're my legal guardian doesn't mean I have to listen to you."

Hannah laughed. "Oh, yes, it does. You're not dropping out. End of discussion."

"You can't stop me." Luke was three inches taller and fifty pounds heavier than Hannah. If he didn't want to go to school, there wouldn't be much she could do to make him go.

She opened her mouth to challenge him, then decided no good could come from arguing her point when he was hungover. Hannah had taken care of others most of her life and at times like this she dreamed of only being responsible for herself.

"I bet Connor's mother would let me live with them."

Not on your life. "Mrs. Henderson doesn't even want you hanging out with Connor anymore."

"Liar."

"You can ask her yourself."

"Why would she say that?"

"Maybe because she caught you two drinking and she thinks you're a bad influence on her son."

Luke laughed, then moaned and pressed his hands to his head. "Connor drank before we started doing stuff together."

"Did Connor talk you into drinking?"

"No. Ben Nichols and I got slammed last year."

"Is Ben the one who gave you the pot?"

"Yeah."

She'd found Luke smoking in the hayloft over Christmas break and had flipped out. He'd been so stoned he was lucky he hadn't started a fire in the barn.

"Maybe you should smoke pot, then guys might like you better." Luke could be downright ugly toward her when he wanted to be. "I bet if you weren't such a nag, Seth wouldn't have dumped you."

Hannah gaped at her brother in the rearview mirror. "For your information, *I* broke up with him."

Seth Markham had caught Hannah at a weak moment when he'd proposed to her following her father's funeral. She'd been in a state of panic after learning about the financial mess the ranch was in. When Seth had promised he and his father would pay off the Blue Bison's debts, she'd decided that marrying him was the only sensible thing to do if she didn't want to lose her and Luke's inheritance.

Seth had pressed her to wed right away but Hannah had needed time to grieve. Three months passed, and when she still hadn't set a date, Seth became angry and they'd argued. He'd almost convinced her to go to the courthouse that day before he'd let it slip that he and his father had planned to sell her bison and expand their cattle herd. Hannah had promptly returned his ring.

"Watch it!"

Startled out of her trance, Hannah realized the truck had drifted onto the shoulder and was headed straight toward a hitchhiker. She slammed on the brakes, then swerved back into her lane—right into the path of a shiny metal object lying on the asphalt. The rear tire blew and the truck fishtailed off the road and down an embankment, where it stopped inches from a barbed wire fence.

"Luke, are you all right?" She craned her neck over the backseat.

Her brother crawled up from the floor. "Shit, Hannah. You could have killed us. Didn't you see that guy?"

She looked out the passenger window. The hitchhiker had dropped his duffel bag on the ground and was jogging toward them. He wore military fatigues and a white T-shirt that showed off his powerful arms and an impressive chest. He had short, dark hair, thick beard stubble covered his face and aviator sunglasses hid his eyes. No wonder he hadn't jumped out of the way—he'd been wearing earbuds.

Luke opened the back door and got out of the truck.

"Everyone okay?" the man asked when he reached them. He took off his shades and ran his gaze over Luke.

"We're good," Luke said.

Hannah joined Luke and said, "I'm so sorry. I wasn't paying attention to my driving. I didn't hit you, did I?"

"Not by a long shot. How about you?"

His eyes were a hypnotizing shade of caramel brown. "How about me what?"

"Did you get hurt?" His sexy mouth spread into a grin. She shook her head. "I'm fine."

He examined the rear wheel. "You've got a flat tire."

Hannah peered over his shoulder. She'd been driving on bald tires for months. It had only been a matter of time before one of them blew.

"If you have a spare, I'll put it on."

Where were her manners? When he stood, she held out her hand. "Hannah Buck." His warm grasp was the nicest thing she'd touched all morning.

"Alonso Marquez."

"This is my brother, Luke," she said.

The males shook hands and Hannah noticed Alonso was only an inch or two taller than Luke's five-ten.

"I have a spare," she said. "Luke, grab the wrench and jack from the toolbox."

Her brother climbed into the truck bed and rummaged through the steel storage compartment, then handed the tools to Alonso.

Hannah closed her eyes and rubbed her brow, where a dull throb beat against her skull. The headache had begun right after she'd picked up Luke from Connor's.

"Hey," a deep voice whispered near her ear, and she jumped. "It's okay." Alonso smiled. "No one got hurt."

Tears stung her eyes at the note of concern in the stranger's voice. When was the last time anyone had been worried about her?

True to his word, Alonso put the spare tire on in record time.

"Thank you," she said. "And I'm really sorry I almost ran over you."

"Be careful." He saluted her before walking back to retrieve his bag.

"Aren't you going to give him a ride?" Luke asked.

"We don't know anything about him," she said.

"Who cares? He helped us, didn't he?"

True, but what if Alonso turned out to be a serial killer or robbed them at gunpoint after she dropped him off farther down the road? Still…this was a lonely stretch of Highway 8 and the town of Paradise was fifteen miles away.

"Hey, mister, you want a ride?" Luke shouted.

Alonso waved Luke off, then put in his earbuds, threw his bag over his shoulder and started walking.

Luke jogged toward Alonso—funny how his hangover prevented him from doing chores but not racing after strangers. Alonso listened to Luke for a minute, then the two walked back to the truck.

"I told him that you were worried he might kill us." Luke nudged Alonso's arm. "Tell her what you said."

Alonso flashed his white teeth. "I don't kill. I save lives."

"He's a doctor, Hannah."

"Trauma surgeon," Alonso said.

Luke nodded to the man's fatigues. "And he was an Army doctor in Afghanistan."

Hannah would never have guessed the sexy, masculine man was a surgeon. "Why are you hitchhiking?"

"I took a personal leave from the University of New Mexico Hospital in Albuquerque." He looked at Luke. "Kid, I appreciate the thought, but your sister's uncomfortable giving me a lift."

Luke jutted his chin. "This truck belonged to our dad, so it's half mine and I say you can have a ride."

Alonso glanced between sister and brother. He didn't care to get involved in their squabble. The teen leaned in close and Alonso caught a whiff of stale alcohol on his breath. "You can ride up front," Luke said.

"Aren't you a little young to be drinking?"

"I'm sixteen."

"Last I heard the drinking age around these parts was twenty-one."

"No one pays attention to that law."

Touché. Alonso had drunk as a teen—not often— but he'd slammed back a few beers once in a while so the homies in the 'hood wouldn't make fun of him. It had been tough enough that the kids had picked on him for getting good grades. If not for his little sister Lea's asthma attacks, forcing Alonso to skip school to care for her while their mother worked, he'd have been a regular Goody Two-shoes. And Goody Two-shoes never made it out of the barrio.

"Stay out of trouble, kid." Alonso left the siblings by their truck and started down the road. He'd walked less than a minute before Hannah pulled up next to him and lowered the passenger-side window. He took out his earbuds but kept walking.

"Where are you headed?" she asked.

"Nowhere in particular." He'd had no plan in mind when he'd left his job—just that he hoped lots of fresh air and escaping the city would restore his faith in humanity. His coworkers thought he'd lost his mind when he'd confessed that he needed a break from the blood and gore. Their disbelief hadn't surprised him. ER doctors and nurses were adrenaline junkies who thrived on chaos. But Alonso's past was catching up to him. He'd grown up in a rough neighborhood, watching bad things happen to good people. His time in Afghanistan was more of the same—good soldiers losing their lives at the hands of the people they were trying to help. Then he'd returned to the States, where he tried to save more lives—kids shot by kids. Women who were beaten by their boyfriends or husbands. Drug overdoses and innocent men, women and children injured by intoxicated drivers. He'd become weary of all the death and destruction and had needed to escape it for a while.

Luke poked his head out the window. "You can stay at our ranch if you want."

"Luke!" Obviously Hannah didn't want Alonso anywhere near her or her brother. *Smart girl.*

"I'm good, thanks." He read the indecision in Hannah's pretty blue eyes and he let his gaze linger on her.

At first glance she came off plain looking, but upon closer inspection he noticed her eyes darkened to indigo when they shone with worry. Her mouth was a little wide and he imagined what it would feel like to kiss her full lips. *Damn.* He'd just met Hannah and already he was thinking of having sex with her. She was smart to be wary of him.

"Luke's right. You deserve a lift after I almost ran you down, and then made you change a flat tire."

"Thanks." The word was out of his mouth before he could stop it—blame it on her baby blues. Once he got situated in the truck bed, the half window in the backseat opened.

"You can sit up front with my sister."

"I'm fine right here." Alonso put in his earbuds but didn't turn on the music. He shouldn't eavesdrop, but he was curious about the siblings.

Hannah guided the pickup onto the road and Alonso closed his eyes against the cool breeze. When he'd begun his journey five days ago the high had been seventy-three. He'd headed southeast and had walked twelve hours a day, covering almost thirty-five miles per day. Each twenty-four-hour period that passed, the temperature had dropped. He guessed the first day in November hovered near sixty-five degrees.

"Why are you so mean?" Luke's accusation drifted through the open window.

"What are you talking about?" Hannah asked.

"Making Alonso sit in the truck bed because you think he's some psycho."

Alonso thought Hannah should be suspicious of him. Not only didn't she know much about him, but he carried a handgun in his duffel bag.

"Leave it be, Luke. I don't want to argue with you."

Luke tapped his shoulder. "Alonso."

"What?"

"You ever rodeo?"

"No, but I've ridden a bucking bronc before." In high school he and his friends, Cruz Rivera and Victor Vicario, had spent time at the Gateway Ranch, where several cowboys had taught them how to bust broncs. It took only a few short seconds in the saddle for Alonso to figure out rodeo wasn't his sport. He'd spent the remainder of his stay at the ranch taking care of the livestock.

"I want to learn how to ride broncs," Luke said.

"Bronc riding can be tricky."

"But rodeo is so cool."

Alonso sensed a wild streak in the teen—no wonder his sister appeared stressed out. "Some high schools have rodeo teams."

"School sucks." Luke lowered his voice. "I'm gonna drop out."

"I doubt your parents would approve of you quitting school."

"My mom and dad are dead." That Luke said it so matter-of-factly left Alonso speechless.

The truck slowed, then turned onto a dirt road and drove beneath a wooden arch with the words *Blue Bison Ranch* painted in white across it. He should remind Hannah to stop and let him out, but the words never came.

She drove a quarter mile before he saw a house, barn and corral. The place could use a little TLC. The adobe-style home needed a fresh coat of beige paint, and the red barn had faded to pink and was missing a few boards. A flatbed trailer half-loaded with hay bales sat beneath the open barn loft. No ranch hand appeared to greet them—maybe the hired help was out with the cattle.

Hannah parked in front of the barn and as soon as she and her brother opened their doors, they started in on each other.

"Finish loading the hay, Luke."

"You load it. I'm going to bed."

Hannah grabbed Luke's shirtsleeve. "If you think you're old enough to stay up all night drinking, then you can do a man's work the next day."

"I'm sick of you bossing me around. Go to hell." Luke stormed into the house.

Alonso waited for Hannah's next move, then his chest tightened when she dabbed her eyes with her fingertips. He couldn't stand to see her cry.

"I'll load the hay." He hopped out of the truck bed.

She slapped a hand against her heart and stared at him wide-eyed—yep, she'd forgotten about him. A first for Alonso. He was quiet by nature but a decent-looking man, according to the ER nurses, who repeatedly reminded him of their single status.

"I was supposed to let you off by the road."

"Not a big deal. It isn't that far of a walk." He nodded to the trailer. "Loading hay bales is the least I can do to thank you for the lift."

After a second's hesitation she said, "I need twenty-five more."

"Twenty-five bales it is." He waited for Hannah to enter the house, then went into the barn and climbed the ladder to the loft. As he dropped the bales to the ground below, he wondered if the siblings fought like this every day.

Did it matter? As soon as he finished the chore, he'd hit the road again.

Chapter Two

Hannah stood at her bedroom window and watched hay bales sail out of the barn loft. She was grateful that Alonso had offered to help and embarrassed that he'd witnessed the drama between her and Luke.

True to his word, her brother had crawled into bed as soon as he'd gone into the house. Luke was a spoiled brat and she accepted much of the blame for his self-centeredness. She'd always felt sorry for him, because Ruth had neglected him. Then, when Luke was old enough to do guy things with their father, Joe had chosen to spend his free time with a can of beer rather than his son. So Hannah had babied Luke and now she was paying the price.

The tears she'd held back all day dripped down her cheeks. She wiped the moisture away, assuming her weepiness was the result of exhaustion and worry. She returned downstairs, grabbed a water bottle from the fridge and, ignoring the pile of dirty dishes in the sink, she went out to the barn. Halfway there she froze when she caught a glimpse of Alonso's bare chest. He'd taken his shirt off and his skin glistened with sweat, the muscles rippling when he heaved a bale over his head. The sight of all that masculinity set off an explosion of feminine twinges—erotic little aches that she hadn't experienced in a long, long while.

He disappeared from the hayloft window, then a moment later walked out of the barn, his T-shirt hanging from his jeans pocket. "Almost done." He began picking the bales up off the ground and placing them on the flatbed. The words *US Army* were tattooed above an image of eagle wings and a snake coiled around a rod. He hadn't lied about being a military doctor.

She held out the water bottle.

"Thanks." He guzzled the drink, then sucked in a deep breath.

It was none of her business, but she asked, "How long were you in the Army?"

"I did one tour in Afghanistan before I returned to civilian life."

"Are you originally from New Mexico?"

"Born and raised in Albuquerque." He lifted the bottom of his T-shirt and wiped the sweat off his face. "What about you?"

"Born and raised in Paradise." Four generations of Bucks had lived on the ranch outside the small town—population just a little over two thousand. "My great-grandfather bought this land." But it was Hannah's grandfather who had made most of the improvements—digging the water wells and starting up a bison herd. Sadly her father had run it into the ground.

"Anything else I can help with before I take off?"

"No." She motioned to the flatbed. "You've done plenty, thanks."

His eyes shifted to the house. "Is your brother okay?"

She refused to make excuses for Luke. "He's sleeping off his hangover."

"Does he drink often?"

Was Alonso asking as a doctor or just a guy she'd picked up hitchhiking? "He sneaked a can of beer once in a while before our father died. But last night he got caught binge drinking with a friend."

She waited for Alonso to lecture her on the evils of alcohol consumption, which sadly she was all too familiar with. Instead, he said, "Pull your truck over here and I'll hook it up to the trailer, then you drive and I'll cut the bales and drop them where you tell me to."

She wanted to refuse his help but swallowed her pride. Once Alonso hitched the trailer to the pickup, he walked up to the driver's-side window. "Blow the horn when you want me to toss a bale."

She handed him the wire cutters and work gloves she kept in the truck. After he climbed onto the trailer, she drove off, slowing down when she left the dirt road and entered the pasture. She honked every ten yards. Halfway through her route the bison came over a ridge. After Alonso threw the last bale onto the ground she put the truck into Park and got out.

He hopped off the trailer. "I've never seen bison up close. They're pretty impressive animals."

"My great-grandfather raised cattle. It was my grandfather who switched to bison after he lost an entire herd to disease." She smiled. "Have you ever eaten bison meat?"

"Nope."

"We sell our bison to gourmet food markets, but once in a while a dude ranch will ask to buy one of the animals to keep as a pet. Tourists get a kick out of seeing them."

"How many do you have?"

"My grandfather kept a herd of three hundred then

my father decreased it to two hundred, and right now I have a hundred and fifty." She'd had to sell thirty head to cover the back taxes. Once the ranch was in better financial shape, she intended to grow the herd again.

"Ready when you are." He got in on the passenger side and the musky scent of male sweat and faded cologne filled the cab. She turned the truck around and drove back through the pasture. "I would have been doing this in the dark tonight if you hadn't offered to help."

"You don't have any ranch hands working for you?"

"I can't afford to pay one. If Luke would stay out of trouble and do his share of the chores, we'd manage fine."

"Luke mentioned both your parents are gone."

Gone sounded temporary, not permanent like *dead*. Maybe that was how soldiers viewed fatalities in the Army. His comrades never died—they were just gone. "Our father passed away in a horseback-riding accident and Luke's mother died in a car crash."

"Must be rough, handling all this on your own."

"It's been challenging." She parked next to the barn. "You should stay for supper." Hannah decided it would be best if she and Luke had a buffer between them for a while—otherwise they might say something they'd regret. "There's a cot in the storage room in the barn. You can sleep in there tonight, then leave in the morning."

Luke would love it if Alonso hung around and did the rest of his chores for him. But that wasn't why Hannah had extended the invite. She hadn't been involved with anyone since Seth, and Alonso reminded her of how lonely she was for male attention.

"I could use a good night's sleep and a warm meal."

She opened her mouth to ask where he was headed then changed her mind. Come morning Alonso would gone.

"MY SISTER SAID you're staying the night."

"I'll head out in the morning at first light."

"You don't have to clean the horse stalls."

"Someone has to do it." Alonso tossed a clump of soiled hay toward the wheelbarrow.

Luke climbed the ladder to the loft and sat, legs dangling above Alonso's head. Obviously the kid would rather watch than help. No wonder Hannah was miffed at her brother.

"Where will you go when you leave here?" Luke asked.

"I'm not sure. I don't have any place in mind." He pointed to the wheelbarrow. "Lend me a hand, will you?"

"And do what?"

Alonso set the pitchfork aside and dragged a hay bale over to a stall, then dropped the wire cutters on top of it. "Spread clean hay in the stalls I've already cleaned."

Luke took his time climbing down from the loft. "A marine recruiter came to our school at the beginning of the year," he said, tugging on a pair of work gloves. "He made his job sound like fun. Is it?"

"I wouldn't use the word *fun* to describe my experience."

"Where were you stationed?"

"I spent a month at Fort Hood in Killeen, Texas, before shipping out to Afghanistan."

"Did any of your friends get killed in Afghanistan?"

Man, the kid was nosy. The doctors and nurses at the hospital tiptoed around the subject and pretended he'd spent time on an exotic island, not in a war-ravaged country. "Three of my friends were killed over there."

And the hell of it was Alonso had just saved their lives after a roadside bomb had taken out their Humvee. No one expected them to get blown to pieces in the recovery room when an Afghan medic-in-training detonated a bomb strapped to his chest.

"I thought the war was over."

"It is, but there are still crazies running loose in the country." Alonso didn't want to talk about his military experience. "You almost done with that stall?"

"Yeah."

"Grab another bale and finish this one."

Luke did as he was told. "You got a girlfriend?"

"Don't have time for one." That was what he told his coworkers, but after everything he'd been through, he decided nothing good lasts, so it made no sense wasting his energy on a serious relationship.

"Don't you like girls?"

"I like girls fine." He chuckled. "You always so nosy?"

"I guess. It's just that this place is boring."

"What do you do to keep busy?"

"Not much. My sister doesn't like my friends."

Alonso's mother hadn't approved of his school friends but she hadn't understood that a brainiac kid didn't stand a chance in hell of surviving in the barrio if he didn't have buddies to defend him. Alonso's best friends had made sure he hadn't been picked on or targeted by gangs.

In the end it had been Cruz's rebellious behavior that had got all three kicked out of school and enrolled in a special program to earn their GED. To this day Alonso believed he'd never have become a doctor if he hadn't had the support of their teacher, Maria Alvarez—now

Fitzgerald. Things had worked out for him and Vic. Not so much for Cruz—he'd landed in jail. "Maybe you should make new friends."

Luke ignored Alonso's suggestion and asked, "If you're a doctor, why are you hitchhiking? Don't you have a car?"

"I have a pickup back at my apartment in Albuquerque." He pushed the wheelbarrow past Luke. "I guess I didn't feel like driving."

"You're crazy."

Luke wasn't the only one who thought Alonso was an idiot. When he'd told his coworkers he'd needed a break from the ER they hadn't expected him to hitchhike across New Mexico. "Exercise is good for the brain."

"Then, run on a treadmill."

Running in place didn't work. After Alonso left Afghanistan and returned to the States, he'd believed he'd put all the death and destruction behind him. But more of the same had awaited him in the hospital. "You have any hobbies, kid?"

"My dad taught me how to use a shotgun. I like shooting at targets."

Alonso caught Luke staring into space. "It's tough losing both parents."

"It's not that hard. My dad was a drunk."

Alonso had only just met the teen but he felt a special kinship with Luke. Alonso's father had taken off before he'd entered kindergarten, and he wasn't even sure if his old man was still alive. Once in a while he wondered what his life would have been like if his father had stuck around.

Luke leaned against the side of the stall. "What about you? What did you do with your dad?"

"My father wasn't involved in my life."

"Did you do stuff with your mom?"

"Not really. My mom worked two jobs. It was mostly just me and my sisters."

"Did you guys fight all the time?"

"No."

Luke laughed. "Yeah, right. You were best friends."

"There were times when my sisters drove me nuts and I wanted to pick fights with them, but I didn't."

"Why not?"

"One of them has asthma and if she gets upset she can't breathe." Alonso lost count of the times he or his mother had dialed 911 when Lea had trouble breathing. If they'd had health insurance his sister might have gotten the medicine and inhalers she'd needed to stay healthy, but too often her prescriptions went unfilled because there wasn't any money to pay for them.

"That must have sucked," Luke said.

What had sucked was being forced to stay home from school and take care of Lea, because his mother couldn't miss work. After a while the school refused to excuse his absences and had expelled him.

"How old is your sister?" Alonso asked.

"Twenty-six. She thinks she can tell me what to do all the time."

"Are you talking about me?"

Alonso glanced over his shoulder, surprised Hannah had sneaked up on them. He hadn't heard her footsteps on the gravel drive.

"It's true," Luke said. "You bully me all the time."

"Hey, I'm your guardian. I have to ride herd on you, or you'll end up in a heap of trouble one day."

Hoping to prevent an argument, Alonso said, "We're

finished with the stalls. What other chores need to be done?"

"Can you drive a tractor?" she asked.

Luke rolled his eyes. "She wants you to cut the hay."

"If it doesn't get cut soon, the cooler night temperatures will cause mold to grow and ruin the crop."

"I can handle a tractor," Alonso said. He'd had the opportunity to drive different military vehicles while stationed in Afghanistan—how hard could a tractor be?

"We've got a couple hours of daylight left. Enough time to cut half the field."

"Sure."

"I'll hook the side rake up to the tractor. I can follow you in the baler." She glanced at her brother. "I need you to stack the bales as they exit the baler."

"Whatever." Luke marched off.

"I can put up with your gnarly attitude any day as long as you're willing to help." Hannah followed her brother out of the barn. Fifteen minutes later, the three of them stood in the driveway next to the equipment.

"I'll ride with Alonso in the tractor," Hannah said. "Luke, you drive the baler out to the field. After I show Alonso which direction to cut the hay, I'll take over driving the baler while Luke stacks the hay."

An hour later, Alonso was making his third turn around the perimeter of the field. Hannah followed at a distance, Luke stacking the square bales in neat sections on the flatbed.

The work was monotonous but peaceful. Out here he didn't have to worry about someone blowing himself up or a young gangbanger staggering into the ER with a bullet in his chest. Alonso checked the side mirrors and saw Luke signaling him. When the baler caught up,

Hannah got out from behind the wheel and approached the tractor.

"We're losing daylight, so we'll stop here. Thanks again for helping us out this afternoon."

"I enjoyed it."

"You're telling the truth, aren't you?"

"Why would I lie?"

Hannah shouted over her shoulder, "Hey, Luke! Alonso likes driving the tractor."

"He's crazy!"

She smiled. "Oh, well, it was worth a shot."

Alonso's breath caught in his throat. This was the first time Hannah's eyes sparkled, and he caught himself returning her smile.

"We'll leave the baler out here and take the tractor to the house. Let's head home and eat." Hannah drove while Luke and Alonso crowded in beside her.

"You don't really like cutting hay," Luke said.

"Sure I do."

"I bet it's not as exciting as being in the military."

"Depends on your definition of *excitement*." Alonso despised movies that glorified war and made superheroes out of men and women who were ordinary people marching off to work each day. "But I get where all this might become a little boring if you grew up with it."

Luke poked Hannah's shoulder. "My sister loves working seven days a week all year long. But I don't want to be a rancher."

Hannah kept her eyes on the path. The rigid set of her shoulders told Alonso that she'd had this conversation before with her brother.

Alonso sympathized with the teen. He doubted Luke

had had much excitement in his life. His parents were no longer alive and his sister was all work and no play.

Hannah parked the tractor by the barn. "We're having leftovers for supper."

"Your chili's gross." Luke stuck his finger in his mouth and made a gagging noise. "My sister's cooking sucks."

"If you don't like the chili, then make your own meal."

"Why don't I take everyone out to eat?" Alonso said. There had to be a fast-food restaurant within ten miles of the ranch.

"You're not buying us dinner," Hannah said.

"I don't care what you guys do. I'm microwaving a frozen pizza." Luke hopped down from the tractor.

"Do you like your chili over rice or plain?" she asked Alonso.

"I'd rather take you out to eat. Save the chili for tomorrow."

Hannah fought a smile. "Luke's being a stinker. My cooking isn't that bad."

Alonso laughed. "Let me take you out."

"There's a restaurant down the road with a great view."

"That works for me."

"You're welcome to use the shower in the house." She walked off and it took a whole lot more effort than it should have to pull his gaze from her swaying hips. It was a toss-up as to whether he was more excited about getting clean or sharing dinner with a pretty girl.

Chapter Three

This isn't a date.

No matter how many times the voice in her head repeated the sentence Hannah couldn't stop feeling a little bit excited about going out to dinner with Alonso. She hadn't been on a date since she'd returned Seth's engagement ring two years ago. She'd been so busy with the ranch and chasing after Luke that she hadn't had the time or the energy to care about her love life.

Sadly, she'd enjoyed the three short months she'd been engaged to Seth—before she'd discovered his motive for marrying her. Seth had been her first serious relationship and he'd spoiled her. He'd taken her dancing, to the movies and brought her flowers for no reason, and she'd soaked up the attention. For a brief while she'd believed she'd found the perfect partner to go through life with. But it hadn't been real for Seth. He'd led her on and had made a fool of her. The experience had left a bitter taste in her mouth and Hannah wasn't eager to rush into another relationship. But there was nothing wrong with enjoying an evening with a good-looking man.

It's not smart to go off alone with a man you barely know.

Gut instinct said Alonso was harmless. He was a

surgeon—surgeons healed people; they didn't hurt them. Besides, she could take care of herself.

She ran a brush through her long hair, then divided the strands into three sections and braided it. After buttoning her Western blouse and pulling on a pair of fresh jeans, she slipped her feet into cowboy boots, then spritzed perfume on her neck and studied her reflection in the mirror. She looked nice but not desperate. *Good.*

When she entered the kitchen, Luke was eating pizza at the table. "I want to get my car from Connor's."

She thought of reminding her brother that the car belonged to her and she only let him borrow it, but she didn't want to start another fight. "I'll drive you out there tomorrow."

"Can I do something later if I can get a friend to pick me up?"

"No." Was he crazy? "I want you to stay in and go to bed early." He needed a good night's sleep, because tomorrow they had to finish cutting the hay and repair the broken fence.

"Where are you and Alonso going to eat?"

"I'm taking him to the Red Bluff Diner." That Luke gave up arguing with her over going out with his friends was odd, but maybe he was more exhausted than he let on. "Keep your phone handy in case I need to get hold of you."

The creak of the bathroom door drifted down the hallway, then a moment later Alonso entered the kitchen, wearing clean jeans and cowboy boots—not the hiking boots he'd had on earlier. His tight black T-shirt showed off his muscular chest, and a hint of his tattoo peeked below the hem of his sleeve. And the beard was gone. Now he looked more like a medical doctor—the ones you saw in TV shows and movies. The only real-life doctor she knew was seventy-four-year-old Doc Snyder, who ran the clinic in town.

Hannah took the pen and notepad she kept on the counter and handed it to Alonso. "Would you mind writing down your cell phone number in case we have an emergency?" She ignored Luke's snort.

"Sure." He did as she asked, then he removed his wallet from his back pocket. "Keep this business card." He handed it to Hannah.

Juan Alarez Ranch For Boys.

Alonso grinned at Luke. "If we don't come back, call that number. Riley Fitzgerald's been a friend of mine for a long time."

"I told you my sister thinks you're a serial killer," Luke said.

Hannah rolled her eyes. "If you two are finished making fun of me, then—"

Alonso's cell phone rang and he checked the number. "Speak of the devil… Will you excuse me a minute? I have to take this call.

"Hey, Riley." Alonso retreated down the hallway and stopped by the front door.

"Didn't I warn you about ignoring Maria's phone calls?" Riley chuckled.

"I'm sorry. I've been busy."

"Apparently not too busy. Maria phoned the hospital and they said you'd taken a leave of absence. What's going on?"

Alonso swallowed a groan. "Everything's fine. I needed a break from the ER, that's all."

"Why don't you visit the ranch? We could use an extra hand with the boys."

"Thanks for the invite. I'll think about it." With all the bad in the world, Riley's call reminded Alonso that there were a few good people left who gave a damn about helping the less fortunate.

"Don't know if Maria told you or not, but we built a new medical clinic at the ranch."

"Don't tell me she's putting Band-Aids on the kids in addition to teaching school."

"Not anymore. We hired a full-time nurse. As a matter of fact, she's married to Cruz."

"Cruz is out—" Alonso glanced down the hallway, making sure he was alone "—of prison?"

"I would have mentioned it sooner, but I thought Cruz might want to be the one to tell you and Victor."

He wasn't surprised his friend hadn't contacted him to let him know he'd been paroled. Alonso had visited Cruz in prison before he'd headed off to college. He was ashamed to admit that he hadn't thought of Cruz often during the past twelve years—he'd been too wrapped up in his own life and struggles.

"Cruz and Sara married a month ago. He's mentoring the boys and teaching them rodeo."

"Sounds as if things are looking up for him." Alonso wished his life was going as well.

"He'd love to see you."

Alonso wasn't so sure about that. He'd only heard about the night Cruz had been arrested, and he still felt guilty that he hadn't gone along with him and Vic when they'd confronted the gang leader who'd been banging Vic's sister. Maybe if he had been there, he could have done something to defuse the situation and Cruz wouldn't have ended up in prison.

"What are you doing now?" Riley asked.

"Sightseeing." That was the truth. Since leaving Albuquerque he'd seen a lot of *rural* sights.

"You sure everything's all right?"

Riley had the uncanny ability to sense when Alonso or one of his friends was lying. "I'm fine."

"If you say so. Be sure to give Maria a call soon."

"I will. Tell her I said hello."

"Will do. Keep in touch."

Alonso disconnected the call, then returned to the kitchen. "See you later, Luke." He held the door open for Hannah, then they walked to the pickup. "The days are warm but the nights are growing cooler," he said.

"I wonder when we'll get our first dusting of snow?"

That was the extent of their conversation until they reached the highway and curiosity got the best of Alonso. "You and Luke don't have any other siblings or relatives to help with the ranch?"

"It's just the two of us."

"I have two sisters. Carla lives in Phoenix. She's been divorced twice but doesn't have any kids. Lea's married with two boys. Recently my mother moved to Santa Fe to be closer to Lea and the grandkids."

"And your father?"

"He took off when I was little."

"Do you keep in touch with your sisters?"

"We talk every few months." He'd phoned his sisters when he'd returned from Afghanistan but had passed up their invites to visit. He wasn't ready to answer their questions about his time in the military.

Hannah slowed the truck when she passed a fifty-five-mile-per-hour speed sign. "Red Bluff Diner isn't far from here." The road forked and she drove west. "I recommend the bison steak fajitas."

"What about regular beef?"

"They have that, too, but it's not as tasty." She smiled. "Try the bison."

"I'll think about it."

"Mind if I ask you a personal question?"

"Go ahead," he said.

"What's up with the hitchhiking? It's not every day you come across a trauma surgeon thumbing his way through New Mexico."

"I needed a break from all the chaos in the ER." He winked when she looked at him. "They don't call it *trauma* for nothing."

"I thought all you military guys loved working under pressure. Taking a long walk can't be near as exciting as saving lives."

Saving lives only mattered if the people remained alive. "I like the fast-paced atmosphere of the ER, but the constant stress drains your energy."

"How long do you plan to keep walking?"

"Don't know yet." Long enough to clear his head of all the bad memories stored in his brain.

She flashed a teasing smile. "You should have driven, then you'd see more of the countryside."

"I saw enough countryside in Afghanistan to last me a lifetime." Then he'd returned to the barrio in Albuquerque—another war zone, just different people and different reasons for killing each other. "What about you?" he said. "Did you always want to be a rancher?"

"I wanted to go to college, but things were crazy at home and someone had to be there for Luke."

It occurred to Alonso that Hannah had been taking care of her brother most of her life. "What would you have studied if you'd gone to school?"

"I'm not sure. Maybe history."

"Seriously?"

"Go ahead and laugh. I have no idea what kind of job I would have gotten with a history degree but I would have enjoyed taking all those classes."

"I never pictured a woman being a rancher."

"I never thought I'd be managing a ranch, either. But life throws you curveballs, and when I was forced to assume more and more responsibility, I grew attached to the land and the animals. And now I can't see myself doing anything else."

Hannah steered the pickup into a gravel lot and parked. The diner sat on the edge of a bluff overlooking a valley. Spotlights shone across the landscape, which was made up of broken mesas.

"Nice view," he said.

"We'll ask for a table with a view."

When they entered the establishment, an older woman in Native American clothing greeted them. "Hello, Hannah."

"Betsy." Hannah nodded to her dinner date. "This is my friend Alonso. Betsy's father owns the restaurant."

"You've got a million-dollar view here," he said.

"Follow me." Betsy led the way to a table by the windows.

Alonso held out a chair for Hannah, then sat across from her. Betsy filled their water glasses and asked if they'd like to view the drink menu. Hannah ordered a glass of red wine and Alonso a beer. "It feels as if we're sitting on the edge of a cliff."

"Too bad it's dark," she said. "On a clear day you can see the Sandia Mountains from here." When Betsy delivered their drinks, Hannah raised her wineglass. "To helpful strangers."

He tapped the neck of his beer bottle against her glass. Hannah was the first person in longer than he remembered who he felt relaxed with—unlike his co-workers, who were high-strung and neurotic.

Hannah signaled Betsy over to their table. "Alonso has never eaten bison. I thought we'd try an appetizer first."

"The nachos?" Betsy asked.

Hannah nodded. "I promise," she said to Alonso. "These will be the best nachos you've ever eaten."

Ten minutes later Betsy delivered the appetizer and Alonso experienced his first taste of bison. "This is good."

"Told you so." Hannah licked her fingertip and Alonso couldn't tear his gaze from her mouth. Her lips spread in a smile.

"You've got a dreamy look on your face," she said. "What are you thinking?"

"I'm thinking that I'd like to—" *kiss you* "—order the bison burger."

"That's what I'm having."

A surge of testosterone swept through Alonso's bloodstream. He hadn't experienced such sharp arousal since he couldn't remember when. He'd gone on a few dates with nurses when he'd joined the hospital staff, but grew tired of always talking about the things that had happened on their shift—none of them had a life outside of the hospital.

"Did you like the nachos?" Betsy asked Alonso when she picked up the empty platter.

"They were fantastic," he said.

"We'll both have the bison burger," Hannah said. "Make mine medium well, please."

"The same for me." Alonso handed Betsy his menu.

The burgers came out a few minutes later along with a special house-made barbecue sauce. After his first bite, he moaned. "I'll never turn my nose up again when anyone mentions bison meat."

Over dinner he and Hannah chatted about places they wanted to visit in the future. Favorite sports teams—Hannah was a big football fan and cheered for the Dallas Cowboys. They chatted about TV shows and movies—even the latest books they'd read. Not one time did the subject of gangs, murder, shootings or rape come up as it did when he socialized with the hospital staff. Hannah was a breath of fresh air.

"I'm glad you almost ran me over today."

Her eyes rounded and he laughed. "It's been a while since I've had such a charming dinner date."

Pink color stained her cheeks. "I haven't been out for supper in way too long."

Over an hour later, Betsy delivered the check to their table. Alonso paid in cash and left a hefty tip. He didn't want to return to the ranch and end the evening—not when he knew he had to leave in the morning. "Is there somewhere we could stop for a nightcap…maybe dance?" he asked when they left the restaurant.

"There's a dive bar up the road."

"Let's go." He held open the truck door for Hannah and they took off.

Dive was too nice a word to describe the double-wide Hannah parked in front of five minutes later. A pair of motorcycles and a 1995 Cadillac Eldorado sat outside Maloney's.

"You sure this is a bar?" he asked.

"I'm sure."

Once they were inside, Alonso was pleasantly surprised. The owner had torn down the interior walls, creating a large open space. The bikers and an older man sat at the five-stool bar to the right of the door. The rest of the room was filled with mismatched tables and chairs. A jukebox sat in the corner and a sign above a door at the opposite end of the trailer advertised a unisex bathroom. Neon beer signs and No Smoking posters decorated the walls.

"What would you like to drink?" he asked.

"Rico only serves beer or whiskey," she said. "I better stick to beer."

Hannah walked off to pick out a place to sit. He paid for their drink order, then carried the beers to the table.

"Thanks." She swallowed a large gulp before setting her bottle down. Her eyes darted around the room. Maybe she was nervous.

"When was the last time you went out for a drink?" He really wanted to know when she'd last been on a date.

"I can't remember. Do you go out often?"

"Sometimes after a long shift, the staff will head over to a bar near the hospital." He'd tagged along the first few times but after that he'd bowed out, preferring to unwind in his quiet apartment in front of the TV.

"Blue Eyes" came on the jukebox, and Alonso said, "Willie's singing your song." He took Hannah by the hand and led her to the dance floor, where he pulled her close. She smelled sweet and fit in his arms perfectly. When she leaned into him, his body hardened at the contact. He thought about putting a few more inches between them, but Hannah snuggled closer, her pelvis brushing against his hardness. He buried his nose in her hair, thinking he could hold her like this for hours—just the two of them with Willie singing in their ears.

"Well, well, well."

Alonso stiffened and Hannah stepped away from him.

"What are you doing here, Seth?" she asked.

"I saw your pickup out front and thought you were drinking alone." He nodded to Alonso. "Who's this guy?"

"Alonso, this is my neighbor Seth Markham. He and his father own the Los Pinos Ranch."

Seth squeezed Alonso's hand. "I'm also Hannah's ex-fiancé."

Interesting that Hannah had left that tidbit of information out during their dinner conversation. "Nice to meet you."

"What business brings you to Paradise?" Markham asked.

"Just passing through." Alonso slid his arm around Hannah's waist. Markham's eyes narrowed—for a guy who no longer had a claim on Hannah, he acted jealous.

Alonso wasn't in the business of provoking people but Markham rubbed him the wrong way. He moved his hand from Hannah's waist to right beneath her breast and swallowed a chuckle when Markham's face grew red.

"How long are you *just passing through* for?" Markham asked.

Alonso stared at Hannah. "Haven't decided yet."

"We were about to call it a night," Hannah said.

Markham followed them out. "Where are you staying, Marquez?"

"At the ranch," Hannah said, then took Alonso's hand in hers and they walked across the parking lot.

"I'll drive," Alonso said. Hannah offered the keys after he helped her into the passenger seat. He slid behind the wheel and took off. When he glanced in the rearview mirror Markham was standing in the parking lot. "Your ex seemed surprised you were with another guy."

"Seth thinks he can change my mind about marrying him."

"You want to talk about it?"

She was embarrassed to admit how naive she'd been to believe Seth had really cared about her. Thank goodness he'd shown his true colors before they'd walked down the aisle.

"A week after I broke off our engagement, I saw Seth with another woman." On the heels of her anger came hurt then relief. In the end she knew she was better off without him, but it stung that Seth had only been using her. "I was on my way to get Luke from school when I saw him walk out of Maloney's with a redhead clinging to his arm. On the drive back through town I spotted his truck at a motel." She shook her head. "I may be a simple country girl, but even I know the only reason you check into a motel at three o'clock in the afternoon is to have sex."

"You're better off without him."

Hannah offered him a smile. "If your medical career doesn't work out, you'd make a good cheerleader."

Conversation ceased when Alonso turned onto the dirt road that led to the ranch. He parked by the house but made no move to get out of the truck. "If my staying tonight is going to cause problems for you…"

"By problems you mean gossip?"

"I don't want people to think badly of you because

you allowed a hitchhiker to spend the night on your property."

"You're not a hitchhiker. You're a surgeon." *And a darn good-looking one at that.* "I don't care what anyone says about me." Besides, her family had been the topic of gossip for years in Paradise. Alonso would give them something new to chat about.

She glanced at the dark house. "Luke must be in bed." For once he'd taken her advice.

"Hangovers will do that to you." Seconds ticked by, then Alonso reached across the seat and brushed a strand of loose hair from her face. She didn't want the night to end. Didn't want to leave his side.

"Alonso?"

"What?"

"Do you ever get lonely?" Until she'd sat across the table from him at the restaurant, Hannah hadn't consciously acknowledged the depth of her loneliness.

"Yes." His whispered answer made her heart pound. *This is crazy. You hardly know the man.*

She couldn't argue with the voice in her head, but the strength to resist a night in Alonso's arms had fled the instant he'd pulled her close on the dance floor. "I don't want to be alone tonight," she whispered.

He slid his hand around the back of her neck. "I don't want to be alone, either."

And then he kissed her.

Chapter Four

Alonso squeezed Hannah's hand as they walked away from the pickup. A barn wasn't the most romantic place a guy could make love to a woman, but tonight wasn't about romance. When Hannah had looked into his eyes on the dance floor at Maloney's, he'd recognized the pleading glimmer in her gaze. He'd seen the same haunting look in patients who'd stared up at him in pain right before they went into surgery. Hannah didn't want to be alone tonight, and he didn't care to examine why *he* didn't want to be alone, either. He and Hannah were consenting adults and there was nothing wrong in reaching out to each other for comfort.

"There's a cot and blanket back here," she said, leading him past the horse stalls. When they reached the storage room, she flipped on the light.

Alonso took one look at the narrow cot and said, "Not here." He grabbed the blanket and they walked over to the ladder leaning against the hayloft. "You first."

He followed her up, making sure she didn't slip, the swish-sway of her fanny taunting him. They spread the blanket over a soft pallet of hay, then sank to their knees. The loft was warm and the earthy smell combined with Hannah's sexy perfume made Alonso's head spin. He removed the band at the end of her braid, then loosened the strands until the kinky tresses cascaded over her shoulder. He brought a handful of her hair, still damp from her shower, up to his face and breathed deeply. He had no idea why their paths had crossed, but Hannah was good, kind and sweet, and in her arms he knew he'd forget all the bad in the world that stalked him—at least for a night.

He opened his mouth to tell her how much he wanted her, but she pressed her finger against his lips and shook her head. The silent message in her eyes begged him not to make any promises. Tonight was all she wanted from him.

They undressed each other—one button, one zipper at a time. Her boots and jeans, then his. He slid her shirt off her shoulders, kissing each inch of exposed skin. The material bunched at her wrist and with her arms trapped by her sides, he trailed his finger over the swirls of lace on her bra. Her breath caught, then her eyelids closed. She moaned when he cupped her breast and the sensual sound released a wave of testosterone through his body.

"Wait." Her fingers clamped down on his wrist.

His heart thudded loudly in his ears, and he worried she'd changed her mind. She got to her feet and walked across the loft, then unlatched the door and pushed it open. Light spilled across the blanket, and when she returned and stretched out beside him, her skin shimmered in the sliver glow of the moon.

He removed her bra, tossing it somewhere behind him. He took his time pleasuring her, nibbling, licking the soft mounds. Her fingers sneaked inside the waistband of his briefs, robbing him of what little self-control he possessed.

Hannah might be sweet but she knew what she needed from him and he intended to deliver. They removed the rest of their clothing and he kissed her, deep and slow. Arms and legs became tangled as they lost themselves in the magic of the night.

A DULL PAIN shot up Alonso's arm, dragging him from a deep slumber. He didn't have the energy to open his eyes and his foggy brain struggled to register the weight pressing against him. The heaviness wiggled and a soft sigh reached his ears, then he remembered—Hannah. He slid his arm free from beneath her, his fingers tingling as the circulation returned to his hand. She snuggled closer, sliding her leg between his thighs, and he caressed her back, trailing his fingers over her spine and sexy backside.

He closed his eyes, believing Hannah was a miracle drug. He'd hooked up with a couple of women after he'd returned from Afghanistan and neither one had made him feel renewed. Hannah's touch had flushed out the ugly side of humanity and replaced it with a sense of hope and peace.

He'd become a trauma surgeon because he wanted to save people's lives—but medical school hadn't prepared him for the toll that all the violent injuries would take on his soul. The tragedies followed him home after his shift, sneaking into his bed and haunting his sleep. But tonight, after Hannah had drifted off in his arms, he hadn't dreamed at all.

He closed his eyes, feeling serene. Content. Maybe he hadn't needed to walk a thousand miles to clear his head—maybe he'd just needed to walk until he'd found Hannah.

Nothing good lasts forever.

With that thought in mind, he kissed her temple, hoping to rouse her from sleep. He needed her again.

She scratched her toe against his calf. "You're awake."

"Are you?"

She rolled on top of him, her hair falling across his face. "I am now." She pressed kisses to his nose, forehead and chin. He chuckled.

"What's so funny?"

"I'm not used to a woman taking the lead." He felt her smile against his neck.

"I'm not a woman who waits for a man to rescue her." She playfully bit his shoulder. "I can do anything a man can and then some."

She'd get no argument from him. He held her face and brought her mouth to his. "You can take the lead anytime." He gave himself over to Hannah and her healing touch. This time their lovemaking was slow and gentle. The stars were no longer visible in the sky when he closed his eyes and drifted into another dreamless sleep.

WHEN HANNAH WOKE in the hayloft, she was alone. She stretched on the blanket, twitching at the bits of hay poking her skin. Then she smiled—a smile that blossomed deep inside her.

Alonso had been just what the doctor ordered.

Her smile grew wider. She knew what she'd done with him had been out of character, but if she was going to have a one-night stand, she couldn't have picked a better man. She could justify her actions all she wanted—she was stressed out, lonely, whatever. But the truth was, if she'd met Alonso when her life hadn't been so crazy, she'd still have been wowed by him.

Hannah didn't completely understand the attraction—they had nothing in common. He was city. She was country. He was college educated. She wasn't. He saved lives. She was just trying to save her brother. He led an exciting life. She didn't. But none of that had mattered last night.

All good things had to come to an end, and even though she'd rather spend the day in the loft with Alonso, she had chores to do. She dressed, then hurried from the barn. When she entered the house, the smell of frying bacon greeted her nose. Alonso stood in front of the stove, stirring a mountain of scrambled eggs in her cast-iron skillet. Their gazes clashed, then his brown eyes roamed over her disheveled state and his lips curved in a smile.

"You have a piece of hay stuck in your hair."

She brushed her snarly tresses out of her eyes and searched for something to say.

"I didn't want to wake Luke to take a shower in his bathroom," he said. "So I used yours."

"I'll be right down." She raced upstairs, took a quick shower, then changed clothes. On her way back to the kitchen she stopped outside Luke's door and knocked. She waited for his usual "go away," but this morning she got no response. She opened the door and poked her head inside the room. His bed was still made and his cell phone sat on the dresser. Where had he gone? Better yet, how long had he been gone?

"Did you see Luke this morning?" she asked when she returned to the kitchen.

"Isn't he sleeping?" Alonso divided the eggs between three plates.

"No. It doesn't look as if he slept in his bed." Guilt tore through Hannah. If she hadn't been wrapped up in Alonso last night—literally—she'd have gone into the house and checked on Luke when they'd returned from Maloney's.

"Have you tried his cell phone?"

"He left it on the dresser." A ploy Luke used when he didn't want Hannah knowing where he was. "I bet a friend picked him up last night." She doubted it had been Connor, which left one other suspect—Ben Nichols.

"Have you checked your phone for messages?" Alonso asked.

"Good idea." She took her cell from her purse and entered the pass code, then breathed a sigh of relief. "Someone left a voice mail." As she listened to the recording, her legs grew weak and she sank into the chair at the table.

"Hannah, this is Sheriff Miller. Come into the station when you get this. I have Luke here."

Dear God, what kind of trouble had her brother got into this time? She'd warned him to straighten up, but had he listened to her? *No.* She set the phone down. "That was Sheriff Miller."

Alonso's eyebrows lifted.

"Luke's at the jail."

Alonso moved behind her chair and massaged her shoulders. The tender act brought a lump to her throat. "Is he okay?"

"I assume so, or Sheriff Miller would have said something." If only Alonso's gentle touch could wash away her fears. Fear that she was failing Luke. She wanted so badly for her brother to succeed—why was he rebelling?

"Did the sheriff say what happened?"

"No, but I'll find out soon." The eggs on the plate in front of her began to blur.

Alonso knelt next to her chair and tipped her chin until she looked him in the eye. "If you want, I'll go with you to see the sheriff."

Her gaze shifted to his duffel bag by the door. She was dragging Alonso into her problems again, but she was so tired of handling Luke on her own. "You wouldn't mind?"

"Let's go." He dumped the eggs back into the skillet, then slid the pan into the fridge.

Alonso drove and Hannah sat in the passenger seat, trying not to worry—fat chance. All she'd done the past two years was worry. If she hadn't let her ego get the best of her last night, they'd have stayed home and eaten chili and Luke wouldn't have been able to sneak out of the house.

Alonso parked in front of the jail and they went inside. Sandy—part-time secretary and part-time dispatcher— sat at her desk talking on the phone. She pointed to the sheriff's door, then cupped her hand over the mouthpiece. "He's expecting you."

When Hannah and Alonso entered the office, the sheriff set aside a file he'd been reading and stood. "Hannah." He eyed Alonso. "I don't believe I've seen you around town before."

Alonso shook hands with the lawman. "Alonso Marquez."

The sheriff's gaze swung to Hannah, and when she

didn't offer an explanation for Alonso's presence, he said, "Have a seat." He cleared his throat. "Luke's in hot water."

Hannah swallowed hard and prayed her fear that she wouldn't always be able to save Luke's butt hadn't finally come true. "What did he do?"

"He didn't commit the crime but he was with the troublemakers who did."

"Crime?" The word squeaked past Hannah's lips.

"The convenience store was robbed at 2:00 a.m. this morning. Luke sat in the car while the other two boys held the clerk up at gunpoint."

Hannah gasped. She'd been prepared for petty theft or even slashing someone's tires, but not armed robbery. "What are the names of the boys?" And why weren't their parents here?

"The gun belonged to Kenny Potter. He and his buddy T. J. Templeton are both from Cañon City. High school dropouts with rap sheets a mile long."

She'd never met the boys and Luke had never mentioned their names, but she had a feeling they were responsible for her brother suddenly wanting to quit school. "Was anyone hurt?"

The sheriff shook his head. "Maybe it's time to call in social services, Hannah. I know you're trying your best, but Luke may be too much for you to handle alone."

No way would she allow her brother to be put in a group home or sent to live with a stranger.

"I had planned to phone you tomorrow to discuss another situation that came up with him, but now is as good a time as any."

Hannah braced herself for more bad news.

"Matt Connelly stopped by my office to chat on Friday."

Hannah looked at Alonso. "Mr. Connelly is the principal at the high school."

"Luke skipped classes again on Friday," the sheriff said.

She hadn't known. Usually the school sent out automated messages when students didn't show up and their absence hadn't been reported by a parent or guardian. Hannah had never got the message.

"That makes eleven days in two months."

"Eleven?" She only knew about six.

"Matt said the school quit contacting you to schedule conferences, because you never returned their calls."

"I have a ranch to run, but I'm more than happy to speak with someone on the phone."

"That's neither here nor there." The sheriff shrugged. "Matt's hands were tied, Hannah. He had to expel Luke."

Hannah felt nauseous. "Expelled for…a week or two?"

"The remainder of the semester."

"But he'll fall behind the other kids in his grade."

"Some students need more time, Hannah. You and your brother have had a lot to deal with the past few years. People are sympathetic, but if Luke doesn't turn the corner soon, he'll end up in juvenile detention." The sheriff walked out from behind his desk. "I'll get him."

Hannah felt a headache coming on and rubbed her brow. The school and the sheriff blamed her for Luke's wild ways—but that wasn't fair. Luke was sixteen— old enough to know what he was doing. Old enough to know right from wrong. She couldn't beat him into making better choices. He had to do it on his own.

Alonso squeezed her hand. "It'll be okay, Hannah. The main thing is Luke isn't hurt and no one was injured in the robbery."

Hannah clung to his words, wanting with all her heart to believe things would be okay, but she felt as if her world was spinning out of control and she couldn't do anything to stop it.

When Luke walked into the sheriff's office and flashed his I-don't-give-a-crap scowl at Hannah, she had to bite her lip to keep from laying into him. Then he looked at Alonso's sober face and uncertainty filled her brother's eyes. There were a thousand things she wanted to say, but they'd wait until they had more privacy.

"I told Luke that he's used up his last chance. If he gets into trouble again, he'll be processed through the juvenile court system." The sheriff's threat appeared to have little effect on her brother, who stared at the wall, looking bored out of his mind.

"Thank you, Sheriff Miller." Hannah left the office, Luke trailing her and Alonso bringing up the rear. They piled into the pickup, and no one said a word when Hannah drove across the street and parked in front of the convenience store. "Let's go, Luke."

"Go where?"

"Inside to apologize to Mr. Washburn."

Luke grumbled but left the backseat.

Hannah handed Alonso her credit card. "Would you please fill the tank?"

He ignored the card. "I'll take care of it."

She didn't have any fight left in her to argue, so she let him pay for the gas.

"This is stupid," Luke said.

"No. Hanging out with losers and trying to rob a store is stupid!" They entered the business and walked up to the counter. When the manager spotted them, he stiffened. "Mr. Washburn, my brother, Luke, has something he'd like to say to you."

Luke dropped his gaze and shuffled his feet. Hannah set a hand against his back and pushed him closer to the counter. "I'm sorry about last night," he said.

"You're better than those boys you were with, Luke."

Her brother nodded, his face turning red. "I didn't know one of them had a gun."

"Guns kill people," Mr. Washburn said.

"I know."

"I promise you that Luke won't be hanging around those boys anymore." Hannah didn't know how she'd keep that promise but she'd find a way.

"That's good to know." The phone rang. "I need to answer that. Good luck."

Hannah would need all the luck she could get. They left the store, and instead of driving to the ranch, Hannah headed out to the Hendersons' to pick up the Civic. The family wasn't home but the keys had been left in the ignition. When Luke reached for the door handle, she said, "Alonso will drive the car home."

Luke didn't protest while she waited for Alonso to get behind the wheel of the Honda—a gift to Hannah from her father on her sixteenth birthday. She and Luke didn't speak until she parked in front of the house forty minutes later.

"I'll be in my room doing homework." Luke scrambled out of the backseat.

"Don't bother," she said.

His mouth slackened and his jaw dropped open. "You're always telling me to study."

"You were kicked out of school."

"What?"

"Principal Connelly informed the sheriff on Friday that he had to expel you because you've skipped too many days."

"Six is—"

"Try eleven."

Luke scowled.

"The principal will consider allowing you back into school after the Christmas break. Until then you're a full-time ranch hand."

Luke spat a four-letter word, then rushed into the house, slamming the door behind him.

Alonso parked the car next to the pickup. "The change-oil indicator light is on," he said.

Knowing Luke, the light had been on for weeks. "I'll take care of it." Add an oil change to the list of a millions things to do. She opened the driver's-side door of the pickup.

"Where are you off to?" he asked.

Had he forgotten that he'd planned to leave today? "Don't you want a lift back to the highway?"

Alonso's gaze shifted between the dirt road and Hannah. He should leave—put Hannah, Luke and their problems behind him. So why did he feel such a strong urge to stay?

He wasn't surprised by his desire to help them, but he was surprised by his reluctance to leave Hannah. He'd just got a taste of her goodness, and the last thing he cared to do was hike down the road alone.

"I might have a way to help Luke," he said.

Hannah stood on the running board and stared across the roof of the pickup. "How's that?"

"I have connections with the people who run a ranch for troubled teens."

That sounded an awful lot like a group home for boys. "Where is it?"

"Not too far from here. It's called the Juan Alvarez Ranch for Boys. I gave you their card. The guy who runs the place was a former bronc rider. He and Maria helped me and a couple of friends when we were expelled from school."

Hannah's eyes widened. "You were expelled from school?"

"I had an interesting childhood." He grinned. "I can make a call to see if there's room for Luke."

As tempting as that sounded, Hannah couldn't let her brother go off to some boys' ranch without first checking it out. "Tell me again the name of the couple who run the place."

"Riley and Maria Fitzgerald." Alonso hadn't planned on spilling his whole life story to Hannah but she needed someone to help her with Luke. "When I was seventeen, Fitzgerald helped me and two of my friends by convincing a juvie judge to let us do community service at a ranch. While we were there, my high school teacher homeschooled us, and we earned our GEDs."

"There's a school on this ranch?"

"Yep. If Luke went, he wouldn't fall behind in his classes."

"It sounds perfect except for one thing. I doubt I can afford the cost."

"It's free. They're funded through private donations." Money from the Fitzgerald Kentucky Thorough-bred farm.

Hannah stared at the house and Alonso could almost read her mind. She was thinking she didn't stand at chance at preventing Luke from running off again and getting into trouble.

"I need to see this place first," she said.

"I'll ask if we can drive out there tomorrow."

She shut the truck door, then came around the hood and stopped in front of him. "If things work out and they accept Luke, I won't have anyone to help me here."

He'd been hoping she'd ask him to stay. The only thing waiting for him at the end of the dirt road was miles of empty highway. "I'll hang around for a while." Her smile reassured him that he'd made the right decision.

"I'll go warm up breakfast," she said, "while you make that call."

Once Hannah disappeared inside the house, Alonso dialed Fitzgerald's number.

"Change your mind about coming for a visit?" Riley said.

"There's a kid who could use your help."

"Who?"

"His name is Luke Buck. Both his parents are deceased. His sister is his legal guardian, but she's having a heck of a time keeping him in line. He was just expelled from school for the rest of the semester."

"You know we never turn away a kid in need. I'll have Maria get a bed ready in the bunkhouse."

"Thanks, Riley."

"Plan on staying for a while when you come. Cruz will want a chance to catch up with you."

"Sure."

"When can we expect you?"

"Tomorrow."

"See you then."

Alonso shoved the phone into the pocket of his cargo pants and climbed the porch steps. Hannah met him in the doorway. "What did Mr. Fitzgerald say?"

"They're expecting Luke tomorrow."

"Thank you." Her voice cracked and he pulled her into his arms. If he wasn't careful he could get used to holding Hannah.

"It'll be okay. I promise that once you see this place you'll know Luke will be in good hands. When he comes home, he'll be a different kid."

"I hope so." She rested her forehead against his chest.

They stood for a long time, holding each other— Alonso needing her hug as much as she needed his.

Chapter Five

"I don't know why I have to go to this stupid ranch." Luke glared out the passenger window.

Hannah had talked at length with Luke the night before and he hadn't protested when she'd informed him that they were visiting the boys' ranch today. "I promised you that if you don't feel comfortable you don't have to stay." She expected an argument, but Luke turned his sullen face back to the window.

Maybe he was as exhausted as she was. They'd put in a full day's work after rising at the crack of dawn. They fed Buster and the bison, finished cutting the hay. And after storing the bales inside the barn they made temporary repairs to the broken fence—at least the bison wouldn't wander onto the Los Pinos Ranch while they were gone. By two in the afternoon, they'd showered and hit the road. They'd been driving a couple of hours when Alonso left the highway and turned onto a rural road.

"Here we are." Alonso pulled up to a massive gate with the words *Juan Alvarez Ranch for Boys* across the front. He rolled his window down and pressed the green talk button on the security box.

Maria Fitzgerald's voice came over the intercom. "Alvarez Ranch."

"Hey, teach, it's Alonso Marquez."

"Alonso! I can't wait to see you. Come up to the main house." The feminine voice sounded pleasant and Hannah was hopeful this place would be a good fit for her brother.

The iron gates swung open and Alonso drove in.

"Is this a boys' prison?"

"No, but many of the kids here have been involved with gangs, and they want to keep the place as secure as possible."

At the mention of gangs Hannah's positive attitude took a nosedive.

"So I'm hanging out with a bunch of gangbangers from the city?"

"Wait and see. You'll like it here."

Luke gripped the back of Hannah's headrest, leaned forward and spoke in her ear. "I'll get beat up."

"That kind of stuff doesn't happen here." Alonso changed the subject. "You said you were interested in rodeo."

"Yeah."

"One of the best saddle-bronc riders in the country works at this ranch."

"Who?"

"Cruz Rivera."

"Never heard of him," Luke said.

"That's because he rode in prison."

"I didn't know prisons had rodeos," Luke said.

Neither did Hannah.

"Rivera set all kinds of records."

The pickup drove along a steep incline, and when

they reached the top, Hannah's breath caught at the sight below. A white two-story house with a wraparound porch sat in the distance. There were three corrals near a large white barn and white fencing sectioned off parcels of land behind several buildings scattered across the property. Even from a distance, the place appeared well maintained. Alonso parked between a brand-new diesel truck and red sports car.

"Nice wheels." Luke got out and walked over to the Mustang.

The front door opened and two boys with dark auburn hair ran outside. They bounded down the steps and took off toward the barn. A woman with dark hair and an exasperated expression on her face stepped onto the porch. As soon as she spotted Alonso, she smiled and hurried toward him. Alonso met her halfway and gave her a bear hug. "It's good to see you, Maria."

"You look great," she said.

"This is Luke." He put his hand on the teen's shoulder. "And his sister, Hannah. They run the Blue Bison Ranch about a hundred and fifty miles southeast of here."

Hannah shook hands with Maria. "You have a lovely home."

"Thank you." Maria's gaze flicked between Hannah and Alonso, then her smile widened.

Hannah worried that Maria believed there was something going on between her and Alonso. There wasn't. Well, there was but it wasn't... *Never mind.*

"Whose car is that?" Luke nodded to the Mustang.

"Mine." Maria winked at Alonso. "Riley thinks I need to let loose once in a while."

"Doesn't surprise me," Alonso said.

"Luke, there are thirty-seven boys here. I'm sure you'll find a few to make friends with."

Luke didn't appear impressed by the information and Hannah worried he wouldn't give the ranch a fair shot.

"Speaking of boys." Alonso nodded to the redheaded kids playing on the swings with a little girl. "The twins are growing up fast."

Twins? Hannah shuddered. She couldn't imagine having a child anytime soon. Her brother was all she could handle at the moment.

"They're a handful," Maria said. "The little girl is Cruz's stepdaughter, Dani. Did Riley tell you that Cruz's wife, Sara, is a pediatric nurse?" Maria turned to Hannah. "We now have an official health clinic on the property."

"That's great." Hannah was relieved to know that if Luke got injured he'd be in good hands.

"I made up a bed for you in the bunkhouse, Luke. You'll find a backpack filled with school supplies on your bunk."

"Luke brought his textbooks with him," Hannah said.

"Great. I'll chat with Luke's teachers and get his assignments for the remainder of the semester."

"School sucks," Luke mumbled.

Hannah held her breath, expecting Maria to reprimand her brother but the older woman spoke in a calm voice that drew Luke's attention. "We don't have a lot of rules here. But the ones we do have are enforced. You have to go to school each day and you have to complete your lessons. After that you're expected to do your assigned chores. Once those are done, you're free to spend the rest of your day however you want."

That didn't seem like such a bad deal, but Luke didn't agree. "There's nothing to do here."

Maria pointed across the property, where a cowboy walked a horse out of the barn. "Most of the boys here learn rodeo in their free time."

"Is that Cruz?" Alonso asked.

"You won't find a better rodeo instructor than Cruz," Maria said.

Hannah was too far away to make out the man's features, but he walked with a confident swagger.

"Alonso, why don't you introduce Luke and Hannah to Mr. Rivera?" Maria checked her watch. "Dinner will be served in an hour."

"I appreciate the offer to stay for dinner but I'm afraid we have to get back to the Blue Buffalo," Hannah said. "There's no one watching the ranch."

"Well, it was nice meeting you. We'll take good care of Luke. Feel free to call anytime to check up on him."

"Thank you," Hannah said.

Maria returned to the house and Hannah and Luke followed Alonso down to the corral. They stopped a few feet from the pen and listened to Cruz give riding instructions to a boy younger than Luke. Hannah noticed her brother paid attention to every word. Luke might pretend he wasn't interested in the ranch, but Hannah could feel his excitement about having an opportunity to practice rodeo.

The boy climbed atop the bronc, then Cruz stepped back and the chute door opened. The horse leaped into action and Luke moved closer to the pen, his eyes glued to the bronc and rider.

Hannah watched her brother soak in the action and her heart hurt for him. They'd been so angry with each other for so long and she hated that they were always at odds. But she didn't know how to help him. He was sixteen—almost a man—but in her heart he'd always be the little boy who'd been overlooked by his parents. Feeling sorry for Luke had only made things worse when he rebelled. Hannah accepted part of the blame for the situation Luke found himself in. She should have been tougher on him. But it was going to hurt her more than Luke to have to leave him here.

"Watch your hips, Joey! Pull back! Pull back!"

Joey managed to hang on even though he was slipping to the side.

"Look for an opening!" Cruz leaned forward, his body strung tight as if he was the one riding the bronc. "There it is!"

The kid launched himself off the horse and landed on his right shoulder, then rolled to his feet and ran for the rails.

"Good job! You rode like crap, but you nailed the dismount."

Joey flashed a cocky grin. "You wanna challenge me to a ride-off, Mr. Rivera?"

"You wish, kid. Go get ready for supper."

"Yes, sir."

As Luke watched the exchange between Cruz and the teen, the cockiness disappeared from his expression. Maybe her brother would return to the Blue Buffalo with more respect for Hannah—wouldn't that be nice?

"Been a long time, amigo," Alonso said.

Cruz jumped off the rails and shook hands with Alonso. "At least a few lifetimes," he said. A stilted silence followed, then he nodded to Luke. "Who've you got here?"

"Luke Buck, Cruz Rivera."

Cruz shook Luke's hand. "Welcome to the ranch."

Hannah stepped forward. "I'm Luke's sister, Hannah."

"Luke's staying here until Christmas," Alonso said.

Cruz nodded to a rectangular structure behind the barn. "My guess is that Maria already has your bed set up in the bunkhouse. Why don't you go check out your new digs?"

"Sure." Luke looked at Hannah, his brown eyes wide. "Am I gonna see you before Christmas?"

Hannah glanced at Cruz. She wasn't sure if the ranch had rules about visitors.

"Maria usually puts on a big Thanksgiving feast and invites the families of all the kids," Cruz said.

Hannah smiled. "It looks as though I'll be back in a few weeks to see how you're doing." If the ranch wasn't helping Luke by then, she'd bring him home with her.

Luke gave Hannah a hug and Hannah felt her eyes tear up. There was so much good left inside her brother—he just had to find his way back to the kid he used to be. "Behave," she said.

Luke turned to Alonso. "Are you gonna be here for Thanksgiving, too?"

"I don't know," Alonso said.

Hannah expected he'd be long gone from the Blue Bison by then.

"Good luck, kid."

After Luke walked off, both men glanced at Hannah and she guessed they wanted to talk in private. "It was nice to meet you, Cruz." She smiled at Alonso. "I'll wait in the pickup."

As soon as Hannah was out of earshot, Alonso spoke. "Maria said you're married now."

Cruz flashed a full-blown grin—Alonso couldn't remember ever seeing a genuine expression of happiness on his friend's face. "I met Sara right after I was released from prison. Her father owns a restaurant in Papago Springs."

"I hear that's her daughter playing with the twins." Alonso nodded to the swings.

"Dani's father was a doctor who worked in a health clinic in the barrio."

"Was?"

"He took a bullet to the chest when he got caught in the middle of a gang fight involving the Los Locos."

The very gang Alonso and his friends had been pledging before they'd been expelled from high school. Alonso had wanted nothing to do with gangs but they were a necessity in the barrio. Gangs provided protection, and for those really bad off, a place to crash and food to eat.

"I work in the ER at the university hospital. I've seen more than my share of gangbangers come in all shot up."

"You made it through med school. Your dream came true."

"I guess it did." Alonso had confided in his friends that he'd wanted to be a doctor, but a dream like that had seemed impossible for an inner-city kid. "Maria convinced Judge Hamel to write a kick-ass letter of recommendation for me. I think the med schools were afraid to turn me down."

"How did you hook up with Luke and his sister?"

"I took a leave of absence from the hospital. I've been doing some sightseeing in the area and met up with them." Sightseeing sounded better than walking aimlessly across the state.

"Why did you take a leave from your job?" Cruz's direct stare unnerved Alonso. He thought of telling a lie, but his friend would see through him.

"I'm burned out. I needed a break from the death and violence."

Cruz stared thoughtfully, seeing past the wall Alonso hid behind. "I get it." After twelve years behind bars, Cruz probably understood better than Alonso's cohorts. Hell, forget about him. Cruz was the one who deserved sympathy. "What about you?"

"What's done is done. I've moved on."

"Have you spoken to Vic since you got out?"

"No." The one-word answer suggested that Cruz might not have let go of the past. Alonso wished he could help his two friends find peace with each other, but he had enough troubles of his own.

"What's Luke's story?" Cruz asked.

"His parents are deceased and Hannah's trying to keep him in line, but the other night he was involved with a couple of punks who tried to rob a convenience store. This is Luke's last chance to shape up. Next time the sheriff of Paradise promised to arrest Luke if he was caught on the wrong side of the law."

"Is he interested in rodeo?"

"He says he is, but he doesn't have any experience."

"I'll work with him." Cruz glanced at Hannah standing by the pickup. "When are you returning to your job at the hospital?"

"I don't have a definite date in mind."

Cruz looked as if he wanted to ask another question

but they were interrupted by a group of boys leaving the bunkhouse.

"It's chow time," Cruz said. "You coming?"

He shook his head. "I need to get Hannah back to the ranch."

"Will I see you again?"

"You can count on it." Alonso didn't know when, but one day he'd stay for a longer visit. "Keep a close eye on Luke, will you? He's all Hannah's got now."

The men shook hands, then Alonso returned to the pickup and he and Hannah drove off. It would be dark by the time they returned to the Blue Bison. In the morning he'd help Hannah with chores then tell her it was best if he moved on.

Best for whom?

Definitely not him.

"I'M STUMPED." SHERIFF MILLER scratched his head Tuesday afternoon as he stared at the smashed solar panel used to run the water pump on the south side of the Blue Bison.

"At least we know now that my damaged fence wasn't just a Halloween prank."

The sheriff studied the dirt around the fenced-in tank. "The shoe prints look like work boots."

"Does that matter?"

"If the treads came from athletic shoes I'd guess whoever did this was a teenager."

"You don't think the boys who held up the convenience store did this for revenge?"

"Don't see how. They're sitting in the county jail right now." He stared up at the sky as if the clouds held the answers. Then he cleared his throat. "You and Seth getting along?"

Everyone in Paradise believed she'd broken off her engagement to Seth because she'd found out he'd been meeting Mona Montgomery at the El Ray Inn every afternoon. Hannah let them believe what they wanted. "I gave his ring back two years ago. No one holds a grudge that long." Then again, Hannah recalled the mean look on Seth's face when he'd walked in on her and Alonso dancing at Maloney's. The jerk had no right to be jealous. She rubbed her brow, feeling a headache coming on.

"I'll pay a visit to Roger and tell him to be on the lookout for strangers in the area."

"Have you received any other reports of property damage?"

"No. You're the only one."

Hannah didn't like being special.

Back in the patrol car the sheriff asked, "How do you think Luke will do at the boys' ranch?"

"It was tough to leave him there, but it's a nice place and the wife and husband who run it seem to really care about the kids. There's a school on the property and a medical clinic. Luke intends to learn rodeo in his spare time."

"I hope it works out for him." The sheriff slowed the car when the house came into view. "I don't like you being alone out here with vandals running loose."

"I'll be fine."

"I admire you for wanting to keep the ranch going after your father passed away, but it might be too much for you to handle. You and Luke are young. You have your whole lives ahead of you. You should consider selling and starting over somewhere more exciting than Paradise."

This wasn't the first time she'd been urged to sell. After her father's funeral half the land owners in the county had shown up at her door with offers to buy the ranch. Even Luke had urged her to take the highest bid.

Hannah had had ten happy years on the ranch until her father had cheated on her mother. But even though things had changed and Ruth hadn't been much of a stepmother, Hannah had found solace in taking care of the animals and the land. Instead of finding the same comfort, Luke had grown up turning to Hannah for support. She'd hoped Luke's attitude toward the ranch would change, but there was no evidence of that so far.

When they pulled into the yard, Alonso walked out of the barn and waited for them. She'd thought he'd change his mind about staying on to help her, but she was grateful he hadn't.

"I wondered where you were," Alonso said when Hannah stepped from the patrol car. He'd taken the Honda into Cañon City to get the oil changed and had been gone when the sheriff had arrived.

"I took Sheriff Miller out to see the damaged solar panel."

"I'll let you know if I hear anything that might help our case." The lawman closed his window and drove off.

Hannah stubbed the toe of her boot in the dirt. It had been awkward between her and Alonso without Luke around.

"Has the sheriff come up with any leads?"

Hannah shook her head. "I forgot to mention that Maria called yesterday and said Luke's keeping up with his homework."

"That's good."

"I shared with her some of the things Luke and I have been struggling with." Hannah had been embarrassed at how easy it had been to unload on a near stranger, but when she'd hung up the phone, she'd been confident that Maria and her husband would do their best to help her brother.

"Luke's in good hands. You don't have to worry about him." Alonso's gaze strayed to the patrol car in the distance.

He wants to leave, but he doesn't know how to tell you.

She should insist on giving him a lift to the highway. It was selfish of her to want him to stay, but there was something about Alonso that touched her.

You're feeling vulnerable because you slept with him. You would feel this way about any man you had sex with.

Not true. She hadn't felt this connection with Seth.

"Hannah—"

"It's okay." The least she could do was spare him the ordeal of saying goodbye after all he'd done for her and Luke. "I know you're ready to get back on the road to wherever it is you're going."

The look of relief in his eyes socked her in the gut.

"It's not that I don't want to stay—"

"I'll give you a ride to the highway." She didn't want to drag this out any longer than necessary.

"That's okay, I'd rather walk." He was really going to leave.

She panicked. "It'll be dark soon. Maybe you should wait until tomorrow?" *Give me one more night in your arms.*

"I should really go."

You should really stay.

"I'll get you a water bottle." She hurried into the house and gathered several snacks for him, but when she returned outside he was gone. She checked the storage room in the barn. Empty. She stared down the road—nothing. He would have had to jog to get far enough ahead that she couldn't see him from the house.

It was as if he'd been a figment of her imagination. But he hadn't.

Hannah took the food inside, then returned to the barn and removed Buster from his stall. She walked him out to the corral to exercise him. She'd had to sell the other three horses because she couldn't afford to keep them, but she couldn't get rid of Buster. He'd been her father's favorite. She trotted the horse in circles, changing the pace several times as the sun slowly set.

When Buster had had enough, she let him stay in the corral while she changed his water in the barn and added grain to his feeder. Finished with the chore, she went out to retrieve Buster, but froze when she saw Alonso walking back into the yard, his duffel slung over his shoulder. As he drew closer, she noticed his weary expression. He stopped a few feet from her and dropped the bag on the ground. The muscle bunched along his jaw seconds before he blew out a harsh breath. "I can't leave."

Hannah's heart stopped beating.

"Until the sheriff figures out who's messing with your ranch, you shouldn't be by yourself."

Her heart resumed beating in a dull throb. Alonso hadn't returned because he couldn't stand the idea of saying goodbye to her—he'd come back to protect her.

Chapter Six

The first week of November had come and gone at the Blue Bison and the anxious, unsettled feeling that had driven Alonso to leave the ER was slowly being replaced by a sense of calm and peace. The fresh air, physical labor and Hannah's Crock-Pot suppers went a long way in improving his attitude. He sure hadn't expected rural life to make such an impact on him.

Maybe it's not rural life but Hannah that's got you thinking the world isn't such a bad place after all.

Because the third bedroom in the house was used as a storage room for boxes and old furniture, Hannah had offered him Luke's room while her brother was at the boys' ranch, but Alonso had declined the invitation. If he slept in the house, Hannah would do nothing to stop him from crawling into bed with her. He liked and admired her—she was a gutsy woman who cared deeply about her brother and her family's ranch. He didn't want to be the guy who used her to scratch his itch every night then split when it was convenient for him. He and Hannah lived in different worlds and eventually he'd have to return to his.

"Finished in here?" Hannah walked into the barn late Saturday morning with a smile on her face.

"You're in a good mood," he said. She'd worn her hair loose today instead of in her usual ponytail, and his pulse sped up when an image of those silky strands sliding through his fingers flashed before his eyes.

She stopped a few feet away from him and he caught a whiff of her earthy, sweet perfume. She'd left the first three buttons of her blouse open and he had to force himself to maintain eye contact and not stare at her cleavage.

"I think you've shoveled enough road apples. How would you like an official tour of the ranch?"

He'd tour a sewage treatment plant if Hannah was his guide. "Sure."

"Be ready in ten minutes." Then she was gone, her sashaying hips taunting him as she left the barn.

Alonso washed up at the utility sink, then changed into a clean T-shirt. Maybe he shouldn't fight his attraction to Hannah. It was obvious she wanted him, and he was growing tired of walking around with a hard-on all day. They were both consenting adults—if they wanted to have a fling, why couldn't they? As long as she understood that one of these mornings he and his duffel bag were hitting the road.

Hannah and a wicker basket were waiting for him when he got into the pickup. "What's this?" He peeked inside the basket.

"Don't tell me you've never been on a picnic with a pretty girl before?" Mischief sparkled in her eyes.

"My picnic experience is eating Army rations on the dirt ground, but never with a pretty girl." He buckled his belt.

"Then, it's time you found out what you've been missing." She lifted her foot off the brake and drove away from the house. "The water wells are this way." She veered south on the dirt frontage road.

Alonso focused on the scenery—or he tried—but he couldn't stop thinking about how… "Hannah?"

"What?"

"Are you still in love with Seth?" Part of him hoped that she still had feelings for the guy—then sleeping with her would be a lot less complicated because anything long-term was out of the question. "Sorry. I know that came out of the blue."

"I'm not in love with Seth."

"The other night when we ran into him at the bar, it seemed as though he might have feelings for you."

"We've known each other all of our lives but he'd always treated me like a sister or cousin. I was stupid to believe his feelings for me had changed."

"He didn't tell you that he loved you when he proposed?"

"Nope."

"But you went ahead and said yes anyway?"

"I thought I needed help. My father had just died and Luke was acting up." She glanced across the seat. "I didn't know how strong I was until I returned Seth's ring." She stopped the pickup next to a chain-link fence with razor wire around the top. "This well is six hundred feet deep and pumps water from an aquifer to the stock tanks on the property."

"Do you share the aquifer with other ranches?"

"No. That's one reason Seth wanted to marry me. His family doesn't have an underground water source beneath their ranch. If there's a drought, they have to haul water in for their livestock, and at ten dollars per five hundred gallons it gets expensive."

"How many of these pumping stations do you have?"

"Two." She drove toward a rocky incline then parked at the bottom. "You'll love the view."

He carried the basket of food and followed Hannah to the top of the hill. "Hey, you can see the herd from up here."

Hannah spread a blanket on the ground. "When I was in high school, I'd come out here to do my homework."

Once they were seated, she handed him a ham sandwich.

"No news from the sheriff on who's targeting your property?" he asked.

"Not yet." She offered him a water bottle. "How did you end up being a doctor in the Army?"

"I didn't plan on enlisting. Maria Fitzgerald called in a few favors and helped me get an academic scholarship to the University of New Mexico. I talked about going to med school, but didn't think it would happen. Then one day Maria took me to see a recruiter. They offered to pay for my med school if I committed to serve in the military afterward. When I graduated, I was commissioned as an officer and began active duty."

"Where did you do your residency?"

"Lackland Air Force base in Texas. Then they shipped me off to an Afghanistan outpost where they were training local soldiers and police." Alonso didn't want to go into detail about his tour of duty in the Army. He wanted to forget that time—one day in particular— in his life. Besides, his stint in the Army had only lasted a year before he'd been given an honorable discharge.

"Don't laugh, but I've never been out of the state of New Mexico."

"The rest of the world isn't all it's cracked up to be."

He finished his sandwich, then dug through the basket and found an apple.

"Alonso, do you regret what we did in the hayloft?"

The chunk of apple he'd just bitten off flew to the back of his throat and he coughed. "No."

Her gaze landed everywhere but on him. "Is there someone special waiting for you in Albuquerque?"

"You must not think too highly of me if you believe I'd make love to you when I'm seeing someone else."

"Sorry." Her gaze softened.

"The truth…is that I've never been involved in a serious relationship with a woman."

"I'm not buying that. Women swoon over men in uniform whether it's the military kind or a white lab coat."

"I've had a few hookups with women, but for the most part I remained focused on my goal to get through college then med school. Now my work schedule doesn't allow much time for socializing."

Hannah's stare warmed his blood, reminding him that he wasn't working at the moment. When she licked her lips, he gave in to temptation and kissed her. He tasted a hint of mustard and grew hungry all over again.

Her fingers threaded through his hair and pressed against his scalp, begging him to deepen the embrace. He laid her on the blanket and stretched out on top of her, groaning at the soft feel of her breasts against his chest. He rocked his pelvis against her and her fingers reached beneath his T-shirt to stroke his stomach. Like quicksand, Hannah was slowly sucking him under her spell.

A bang echoed through the air and Alonso popped off Hannah. "Was that a gunshot?"

"That's Seth or his father skeet-shooting on their

ranch." Hannah sat up and straightened her clothes. Her hair was mussed, her lips swollen and she looked more beautiful than ever, but the gunshots had broken the romantic spell they'd been under.

"We should head back," she said. He helped her pack up the food. "I need to pick up a roll of fencing wire at the feed store. Do you want to come with me?"

"Sure." They made the drive to the house in silence, Alonso wondering how long before he gave up and caved in to sleeping with Hannah.

When she parked by the back porch, she said, "I'll get my purse and be right back."

While Alonso waited for her, he checked his phone and discovered a voice mail message.

"Dr. Marquez, this is Benson Levanthal. I know we discussed a three-month leave of absence but I've had two doctors quit and we're going to be short-staffed starting December first. Is there any way you'd consider returning before then? I'll need an answer soon."

Click.

Alonso's first thought was that he didn't want to leave. But if he stayed, the attraction between him and Hannah would grow too strong, and then what? Even short flings became complicated when feelings were involved. His boss's call had come at the perfect time. Alonso could be with Hannah in every way he wanted and still have a legit reason to leave at the end of the month.

He could have his cake and eat it, too.

"ARE YOU SUPPOSED to be calling me, Luke?" Hannah had been on her way downstairs after grabbing her purse from her bedroom when her cell phone rang and the number to the boys' ranch came up.

"I get one call a week if I don't have any penalty marks against me," he said.

"What do you mean penalty marks?"

"I get docked if I don't do my homework or I'm late for class and stuff."

He must be toeing the line then if he was contacting her. "I miss you," she said, surprised she really meant it.

He laughed. "You're just saying that."

Hannah couldn't remember the last time she'd heard her brother's lighthearted chuckle, and she smiled. "So tell me all about it."

"I still hate school and doing my homework, but Mrs. Fitzgerald is really nice and she doesn't get upset if you give her the wrong answer. Yesterday we started a chapter in geometry and she let us work in pairs. It's a lot easier when you have someone to help you with the problems."

Hannah sat on the stair step, amazed her brother was chatting about math. He'd never had much to say about school before. "Are you eating?"

"That's going to be the hard part about leaving here," he said.

"What's that?"

"The food's great and I'm gonna have to go back to eating your casseroles."

"Hey, we both know I'm not a great chef. Maybe you can bring your favorite recipes home and we can cook together."

"Cool."

"Have you had any rodeo lessons?"

"Cruz can't let me participate until my first grade report comes out. I have to be passing all my classes."

"When does the report come out?"

"The end of this week. And I made Bs on all my assignments so far."

"Are you excited about riding?"

"Yeah. I get to watch the others and some of them are really good. There's this one guy named Ricky that Cruz says has a shot at making it to the big-time."

The longer Luke rambled on the more Hannah realized how passionate he was about rodeo. When he returned home right before Christmas she'd have to find a way for Luke to remain involved in the sport, especially if it kept him out of trouble.

"Is Alonso still there?" he asked.

"Yes. And I have to say I'm glad. We had another incident on the ranch." Silence greeted her statement. "Someone smashed the solar panel on one of the stock tanks."

"That sucks," he said.

"Tell me about it. Replacing a solar panel isn't cheap. And our property-insurance deductible rose to two thousand dollars."

"What was it?"

"One thousand."

"We should just sell the ranch, Hannah."

"So you've said." She didn't want to end the call rehashing an old argument. "I know you aren't as attached to this place as I am, but we have time to think about our options. You still have two more years of high school."

"Mrs. Fitzgerald said she's going to send you an invitation to spend Thanksgiving Day here. Are you gonna come?"

"Of course. I wouldn't miss it for anything."

"I might get to ride for you."

"Yeah!" Watching her brother on the back of a bronc would be nerve-racking, but she looked forward to seeing him do something that made him happy.

"I gotta go."

"Thanks for calling, and take care of yourself. Be safe and work hard."

"Yeah, I know. Hey, Hannah?"

"What?"

"You be careful, too." Luke ended the call.

Hannah sat for a moment, absorbing the warm feeling filling her. She and Luke had been at odds for so long, and today's call brought back memories of better times between them. Whatever role fate had played in bringing Alonso into her and Luke's lives, she sure owed him a lot. She shuddered when she imagined where things between her and Luke would be right now if he hadn't gone to the boys' ranch.

She heard the back door open and close.

"Hannah?"

She hurried into the kitchen. "Sorry about that. Luke called."

"Everything okay?" he asked.

"Better than okay. He's doing great." She led the way outside and they got into the pickup. "I was worried he phoned to ask me to come get him."

"Glad to hear that wasn't the case."

"For the first time I feel hopeful that Luke's changing for the better." And she prayed the changes would stick once he returned home. She entered the highway and headed toward Paradise.

"I received a call from my boss at the hospital," he said.

"Oh?"

"He wants me to return by the end of the month."

A sharp pain jabbed her chest. If Alonso had to leave so soon then there was even more reason to enjoy what little time they had left together. "Do you miss working in the ER?"

"It never gets boring. Every day is different."

The exact opposite of her life. "As you've seen, here every day's pretty much the same." She flashed a smile. "Except the weather throws a curveball once in a while." Her seven-day week consisted of up at dawn. Feed the bison. Check the water tanks and fence line. Muck the barn. Load hay on the trailer for the next day. Eat. Then go to bed.

"You might do the same things each day but I wish I could experience that comfortableness associated with a routine. Some days I'm so mentally exhausted, I feel gutted."

If she didn't know better, Hannah would believe country life was growing on Alonso.

Only because it's different from his norm. She doubted he'd be content in the boonies for very long. "Don't you miss the excitement of saving lives?"

"Yes and no."

"I get the yes. Tell me about the no," she said.

"I operate mostly on gangbangers who spend their Saturday nights shooting at each other. And I've saved more drunk drivers than their victims." He blew out a harsh breath. "Everything that's supposed to make sense in the world suddenly doesn't when the paramedics push that gurney through the ER doors."

"I can see where that would be a little depressing. But doesn't the good outweigh the bad? Maybe you're saving a gangbanger but you're giving him a chance to turn his life around."

"That sounds nice in theory but that's not reality."

"What do you mean?"

"You don't want to hear the gory details."

"I do, too." When he frowned, she said, "I'm serious." She admired Alonso for dedicating his life to helping others, which made him all the more special.

"Let's just say I've saved several lives where the people ended up dead a short time later, whether through no fault of their own or because they went right back to getting involved with whatever had brought them to the ER in the first place."

"Maybe you'll feel different after this break from the hospital." Hannah sensed he didn't want to talk about his job anymore so she changed the subject. "The drugstore in town has an old-fashioned soda fountain if you want to wait there while I pick up the fence wire."

"Are you kidding? I've never been in a feed store. I have to see what all the excitement is about."

Hannah parked in front of the store, and a cowbell hanging on the door handle announced their presence when they entered.

"Thought you might come in this week." An older man with droopy shoulders stepped from behind the checkout counter.

"Hey, Mel." Hannah motioned to Alonso. "This is Alonso Marquez. Alonso, this is Mel McGinnis. He manages the store." The men shook hands. "Alonso's helping me out at the ranch while Luke's away."

"Heard about your brother," Mel said. "He's had it rough since your daddy died."

Hannah had had it rough, too, but few acknowledged

that. "Luke is fortunate the sheriff is giving him a second chance."

"What brings you in here?"

"Extra fencing wire." She wanted to be prepared if the vandals struck again and tore down a different section of her fence.

"What else do you need?"

"Just the wire. I'll be back in a week or two to buy more horse feed." Unfortunately, she no longer had the money to stock up on supplies. Hannah purchased what she needed when she needed it.

"Be back in a jiffy with the wire." He disappeared inside the storeroom.

"There's some fancy show-horse harnesses in that aisle." Hannah pointed across the store and Alonso went over to examine the tack while she waited at the register. She had opened her mouth to tell him to check out the handmade bird feeders a local resident sold on consignment when the sound of a ladder hitting the floor and a loud thump echoed through the store.

"Mel!" Hannah raced into the storeroom. Mel had fallen off the ladder and lay buried beneath sacks of livestock feed.

"Call 911." Alonso pushed past Hannah and began lifting the feed bags off Mel's chest.

Hannah hoped Mel hadn't broken any bones. She dialed Doc Snyder's number, knowing he could help Mel faster than the paramedics. "It's Hannah, Doc. Are you at the clinic right now?"

"I'm in Albuquerque seeing a doctor about my hip. What happened?"

"Mel fell off a ladder in the storeroom."

"Is he breathing?"

Hannah covered her phone. "Alonso, is Mel breathing?" He nodded.

"Yes, he's breathing," she said.

"Contact the fire department in Cañon City. I'll follow up with him when I return tomorrow."

She disconnected the call then pressed 911 and requested the paramedics.

"How long before they get here?" Alonso asked.

"Cañon City is about forty-five minutes away."

The old man moaned and Alonso placed a hand against his chest. "Don't move, Mel." He didn't want a broken rib to puncture a lung or his heart. He checked for broken bones, starting at the ankle. Everything appeared fine until he touched Mel's shoulder and the man cried out.

"Your shoulder is dislocated." Mel's face turned ashen and his breathing grew rapid and shallow. Alonso worried the old man would go into shock if he didn't get the pain under control. "I need to put your shoulder back in place." Then he could wrap the joint in ice and numb the pain, which hopefully would help Mel's blood pressure return to normal.

Hannah knelt on the other side of the old man. "Alonso's an ER doctor, Mel. You can trust him."

Mel nodded, then closed his eyes.

"Squeeze as hard as you want," Hannah said, holding Mel's hand in both of hers.

Being as gentle as possible, Alonso worked the frail bone back into place, then said to Hannah, "Find some ice and an elastic bandage if you can." After she left the room, Alonso checked Mel's pulse. Slow but steady. He felt the man's rib cage. "Does it hurt to breathe?"

"A little."

"You need to have your ribs X-rayed."

Hannah returned with a bag of ice from the machine outside on the porch and Vetrap horse-bandaging tape. Alonso opened the ice, poured half in the trash can, then tied off the end of the bag. He moved Mel's arm so it rested across his stomach, then secured the bag of ice to his shoulder with the wrap.

"Maybe you can find a blanket and something to use for a pillow," Alonso said.

Hannah grabbed a handful of saddle blankets from the shelf and Alonso made Mel as comfortable as possible, but it was obvious by the old man's grimace that he was in a lot of pain. "How long have we been waiting?"

"Thirty-five minutes."

Alonso heard the faint wail of a siren in the distance. "They're almost here, Mel," he said.

When Fire and Rescue showed up, they took Mel's vitals then started an IV.

"Mel." Hannah spoke close to his ear. "I'll call Harriet and have her meet you at the hospital in Cañon City."

Mel lifted his uninjured arm and Alonso held his hand. "Thank you, young man."

"My pleasure."

"Don't worry about the store. I'll ask Sheriff Miller to lock up," Hannah said.

The paramedics wheeled Mel outside and loaded him into the rescue truck. After they drove off, Alonso helped Hannah straighten the store. "Will you carry this for me?" She handed him the fencing wire. "Sheriff Miller said he'd be here in a few minutes to lock the store. I think it's okay if we leave now."

Alonso put the wire in the truck bed. "You want to drive?"

"Sure." Hannah slid behind the wheel but before she drove out of town she said, "Things could have turned out a lot differently for Mel if you hadn't been here."

"He's a tough old bird. He'll be okay."

"I know, but I still think you saved the day."

"Hey, I'm no superhero."

She clasped his face between her hands and kissed him. "Paradise has its very own Captain America."

Chapter Seven

"I need to stop at the convenience mart," Alonso said after Hannah drove away from the feed store.

"Sure."

When she pulled into the parking lot of the store, he asked, "Do you need anything?"

"No, thanks. I'll wait in the truck."

Alonso grabbed a large soda then strolled through the aisles searching for the prophylactics. He had two choices: the date-night size containing three condoms or the stud size thirty-six count. There was only one choice for Captain America—he grabbed the bigger box. After Hannah's kiss a few minutes ago he'd decided he was done fighting the attraction between them. She wanted him in her bed so that was where he intended to sleep until he left at the end of the month. But this time he was taking precautions, unlike the night they'd spent up in the hayloft.

When they arrived back at the ranch, Hannah made supper while Alonso loaded the hay bales onto the flat-bed trailer. Afterward he grabbed a clean change of clothes, shoved three condoms into his jeans pocket, then went into the house, where the smell of bacon greeted him. Hannah stood at the sink washing a head of lettuce, her fanny twitching to an oldies tune on the radio.

"Do I have time to shower?" he asked.

She jumped.

"Sorry." He dragged his gaze from her backside. "I didn't mean to startle you."

Her smile more than forgave him. "Supper won't be ready for a half hour."

He lifted the lid on the Crock-Pot. "Smells good."

"Cheesy chicken, bacon and Tater Tots."

"Is this your recipe?"

"Found it on the internet."

He set the lid back in place, then nuzzled her ear. "I think I'll call you my Crock-Pot princess." He left the kitchen, Hannah's stare burning into his back.

He'd just finished shampooing his hair when a cold draft floated across his naked backside. Before he had time to register that he wasn't alone, Hannah's fingers walked down his spine. His breath caught in his chest when she sneaked her hands around his waist then slid her palms down the front of his thighs. When she cupped him intimately, he braced his hands against the shower wall and clenched his teeth. He let her have her fun for a minute, but the need to have her again had been building inside him since the first time they'd made love, and he couldn't wait any longer.

He turned around and reached for her, holding her against him, letting their wet skin rub together in all the right places. "I bought condoms at the store today. They're in my jeans pocket."

"Good." She stood on tiptoe and kissed him.

"Are you sure, Hannah?" He brushed her damp hair away from her eyes.

"Very sure." She pressed tiny kisses across his chest. Her tender caresses made him feel safe. In Hannah's arms he believed he could conquer anything—a heady feeling for a man who'd been fighting a losing battle for a long time.

HANNAH PULLED HER sweater tighter around her as she sat in the rocking chair on the front porch and sipped a glass of wine while she waited for Alonso to return from checking the stock tanks.

Two weeks had passed since she'd joined him in the shower and they'd fallen into a comfortable routine, one Hannah wished could last forever. Alonso woke early and drove the hay out to the herd while she slept in—a luxury she hadn't experienced in years. Then he spent the rest of the day fixing things around the property that she'd neglected because she hadn't had the time or the money to hire someone to make the repairs. And most important, he'd installed the new solar panel she'd ordered for the water station, so now water could be pumped to all the stock tanks on the property.

While Alonso kept busy, Hannah worked inside the house. She'd given the rooms a thorough cleaning, even dusting the baseboards and ceiling lights. Once all the rooms sparkled, she paid bills, balanced the ledger, transferred money from savings to checking, and when the tax bill came in the mail she cashed in the last CD her father had in the bank.

At the end of each day, she and Alonso talked over supper—about everything and anything, except their relationship. After cleaning up the dishes they snuggled on the couch and watched TV until one of them grew bored and began pestering the other. One kiss led to more, and then clothes came off and they made love. Afterward, Alonso carried her to bed, where they fell into an exhausted sleep.

But every morning Hannah woke up in an empty bed—a reminder that their relationship was temporary. After showering she'd fix a fresh pot of coffee, then sit on the porch and wait for Alonso to return from feeding the bison. Some mornings he grabbed a cup of coffee and sat with her, and other times he'd take her by the hand and lead her back up to the bedroom.

The sound of a horn honking drew her attention and she spotted a dust cloud moving along the road. She set her wineglass down and descended the porch steps. As the vehicle sped closer she recognized Seth's pickup. He honked the horn again—this wasn't a social visit.

He stopped the truck in the driveway. "Where's the city slicker?"

Maybe he'd been drinking. "What's wrong?"

"One of our ranch hands tried to rescue a deer caught in the fence and got chewed up pretty bad by barbed wire. He needs a doctor."

"Who?"

"Joseph."

"Why didn't you take him to Doc Snyder or to the emergency room in Cañon City?"

"He's bleeding bad. And since I found him along your property line, I figured it was faster to bring him here and let your *boyfriend* do his magic."

Alonso wasn't her boyfriend, but she didn't bother correcting Seth. She rushed over to the truck bed and winced when she saw the cowboy's bleeding body resting on a blanket.

"I put a tourniquet on his arm, but he'd lost a lot of blood by the time I found him."

"Alonso's out with the herd." As soon as she spoke, her truck crested the ridge and headed toward the house. "Here he comes now."

Alonso parked next to Seth's pickup. "What's going on?"

"One of the Los Pinos ranch hands is injured," she said.

Alonso peered into the truck bed, then hopped over the tailgate and felt for the man's pulse. "Bring me another blanket and a pillow." After Hannah raced into the house, he examined the man's wounds. "What happened to him?"

"Tangled with some barbed wire."

"Where's the nearest trauma center?" Alonso asked.

"Cañon City, but they're doing construction on the road and the detour takes an hour," Seth said.

"He tore the basilica vein on the inside of his arm. It needs to be sutured and he's lost too much blood already."

Hannah returned with the supplies. "Where are we going?" she said.

"Call Doc Snyder and tell him to meet us at the clinic." Alonso covered the man with the blanket and shoved the pillow beneath his head. The cowboy groaned but remained unconscious. Markham hopped back in the cab and took off, and Hannah followed in her pickup.

The sun dipped behind the horizon and a gust of cold wind sent a chill through Alonso. He tucked the blanket tighter around the man. The brisk temperatures reminded him of the night he'd lost three fellow soldiers. Just like the scenarios he faced in the ER, his skill at saving his friends' lives had been wasted that fateful, frigid evening.

The truck hit a pothole and his butt smacked against the bed, jarring his tailbone and his thoughts back to the present. The town lights glowed in the distance as they approached Paradise. Both trucks parked behind the clinic where the back door had been propped open. Alonso checked the patient's pulse—weak but steady.

"What happened?" An elderly man stepped outside, wearing latex gloves.

"Joseph Rodriguez tangled with barbed wire," Markham said, stepping out of the truck. "I had to put a tourniquet on his arm."

Doc Snyder came over to the truck and Alonso got his first good look at the country doctor. The old man's face was as wrinkled as a paper road map—just how old was this guy?

"Doc, this is Alonso Marquez," Hannah said.

"You did a fine job putting Mel's shoulder back in place the other day."

"Thanks." Alonso helped Markham carry Joseph into the clinic and place him on an exam table in one of the patient rooms. Then Doc pressed his stethoscope against Joseph's chest.

"Weak heartbeat. He's lost a lot of blood."

"He tore the basilica vein," Alonso said.

"Hannah said you're an ER doctor."

Alonso nodded.

"Good. I can use your help." He held out a bag of saline and Alonso started an IV in Joseph's uninjured arm. "I'll need you to do the suturing." If Alonso hadn't been staring intently at the old man's hands he might not have noticed the slight tremble. Old age was catching up with the doctor, and it was too risky for him to close the vein—one slight tremor and the doctor would sever the vein wall and the cowboy would bleed out.

Doc nodded to Seth and Hannah. "You two wait in the front room."

Alonso cleaned the blood around the wound so he had a better view of the vein while Doc gave Joseph a shot.

"That'll knock him out for a while." Then Doc handed Alonso a suture kit.

First, Alonso numbed the area with medication, then he worked quickly to stitch the wound closed. He finished in less than a minute.

"Haven't seen anyone close a vein that fast in my entire career."

"I've had plenty of practice. First in the Army and then in Albuquerque at the university hospital."

Doc pressed his fingers against Joseph's wrist. "Pulse is improving. Let's see if any of the other cuts need stitches."

Alonso cleaned and bandaged several wounds on the man's face, neck, arms and hands. Two of the abrasions needed stitches. Then Doc administered a tetanus shot and a round of antibiotics. "He'll sleep for a while." He pulled a chair closer to Joseph and sat.

"Shouldn't he be transported to the hospital?" If the stitches didn't take and the vein opened again, the man would bleed out on the table.

"That's why I'm sitting with him."

Alonso swallowed a curse. What good would it do for Doc to stay by the man's side when he couldn't hold a needle steady? Alonso took a seat in the other chair by the door.

Doc's mouth lifted in a tired smile. "I'm glad you were here, Alonso."

"It's no big deal."

"I couldn't have repaired the vein with my hands. You saved his life tonight."

Alonso had saved a lot of lives, but too many of them hadn't valued their second chance and had ended up dead.

"Joseph's a good man."

"Tell me about him." Alonso was surprised he'd asked the question. He rarely knew anything personal about the patients he worked on.

Doc tapped the gold band on Joseph's right ring finger. "He's the father of five children. His wife died of cancer. Joseph's mother helps care for the kids while he works two jobs."

"That's rough."

"He punches cows during the week for Seth and his father, then on the weekend he's a roughneck for the oil and gas companies." Doc smiled. "His family means everything to him."

Alonso stared at the man's scratched face and the knot in his gut that he'd brought home from Afghanistan with him slowly loosened. It was a good feeling to know that Joseph wouldn't waste his second chance. His gaze wandered around the room. The sparse rural clinic was nothing fancy or as exciting as the hustle and bustle of a hospital ER, yet what he'd done tonight in this small room was on par with what he did every day at the hospital.

Voices sounded in the hallway outside the door.

"Sounds like Sheriff Miller," Doc said.

Knuckles rapped on the door and the sheriff stepped

inside the room. "Joseph's kids are here," the sheriff said. "Can they see him?"

Before Doc answered, five youngsters pushed their way past the sheriff and entered the room. The eldest couldn't have been more than twelve or thirteen.

"Be careful," Doc said. "Don't touch your papa. He's sleeping."

The littlest girl climbed into Doc's lap and stared fearfully at her father. "It's okay, Elsa." Doc patted the girl's back. "Your papa is going to be just fine."

An older woman with a long gray braid falling down her back stepped into the room. As soon as she saw her son she began crying.

Hannah hovered in the hallway, staring helplessly at the sobbing family. The sheriff nudged Alonso in the arm. "Do you speak Spanish?"

Alonso's gaze shifted between Doc, Markham, the sheriff and Hannah—none of them spoke Spanish. So Alonso told Joseph's mother what had happened to him and that he'd be fine once he healed. Mrs. Rodriguez asked how soon he'd be able to return to work, and Alonso advised her that his arm would need to heal for several weeks. The news bought more tears to her eyes.

The sheriff offered to drive Joseph home in the morning, but when Alonso conveyed the message, the older woman asked if she and the children could stay the night at the clinic. Alonso translated their request and Doc agreed then sent the sheriff across the street to pick up snacks for the kids from the convenience store. There was never any mention of who would pay for what.

"Doc, where do you keep the extra blankets and pillows?" Hannah asked. "I'll get them out for the kids."

"The room at the end of the hall," Doc said. "There's a cot in there that I sleep on sometimes."

"Is Joseph going to be okay?" Markham asked.

"He will, but he won't be able to use his arm for a while."

"I'll find him something else to do until you give him the okay to go back to work." Markham glanced at Alonso. "Maybe you can tell him that when he wakes up tomorrow."

"I'll call Alonso in the morning and have him speak to Joseph over the phone before he leaves the clinic."

"Thanks, Doc." Markham left through the back door.

There was no excuse for how the rancher had deceived and hurt Hannah, but at least he wasn't a total ass if he was willing to give his employee a paycheck until the man could work cattle again.

"Would you like me to stay?" Alonso asked Doc.

"We'll be fine," Doc insisted. "Keep your phone by you tonight. I'll call if I need you."

Hannah appeared in the doorway with the bedding. "Tell the kids to come with me and we'll make a fort."

Alonso conveyed the message and the kids followed Hannah back to the front room. Alonso wrote his cell number on a prescription pad and left it on the counter, then went out to the waiting room, where Hannah and the kids were draping blankets over the chairs. The little ones crawled under the covers and Alonso told them to get some rest so their father could sleep, then he told Hannah he'd wait for her outside.

When Alonso left through the back door he noticed Markham's truck still parked in the lot. The driver's side door opened and Markham stepped out. "I've been waiting to have a word with you."

This ought to be good. "Yeah, and what is that word?"

Markham glared. *Too bad.* Alonso had saved a life tonight—that entitled him to be sarcastic.

"I don't know what game you're playing with Hannah, but you'd better not hurt her."

The rancher was one to talk.

"If you try anything with her, I'll—"

Alonso grabbed Markham by his coat collar and shoved him against his truck. The rancher was a few inches taller, but Alonso had been in numerous scuffles during his life and he wasn't intimidated. "What Hannah and I do is our business. Not yours. You had your chance with her and blew it." He released the coat collar and stepped back.

Markham jabbed his finger at Alonso. "I'm watching you, Marquez."

I'm shaking in my combat boots, buddy.

Markham got into his vehicle and sped off.

"Marlene's bringing Doc and Joseph's family supper, and she said she'd stay at the clinic and help watch the kids so Joseph's mother can sit with Doc in the exam room."

"Who's Marlene?" Alonso held open the driver's side door for Hannah.

"Doc's wife." Hannah slid behind the wheel and Alonso sat on the passenger side. She turned on the radio and neither of them spoke during the drive back to the ranch.

Alonso used the time to mull over the events of the past week. He was surprised that he'd felt the same sense of satisfaction at putting Mel's dislocated shoulder back into place as he did suturing Joseph's torn vein. He wondered if the good feeling inside him was a result of whom he'd helped. Mel and Joseph hadn't just been names on a patient chart—they'd been real people. Good people. People family and friends depended on—not people who hurt others.

"I wonder if my Crock-Pot lasagna is still edible," Hannah said when she parked in front of the house.

"I'm hungry enough to eat anything." Alonso opened the door for Hannah. Once they stepped into the kitchen, she hugged him. "Doc said you were amazing and that you saved Joseph's life."

He relished Hannah's hug, letting her warmth seep into his tired body.

"While you take a shower," she said, "I'm going to salvage supper."

Alonso used the shower in Luke's bedroom and stood under the warm spray, letting the water ease the tension in his shoulders. During all the chaos tonight Hannah had remained calm and steady. She hadn't swooned or panicked at the sight of Joseph's bloody body. She'd make a great doctor's wife.

After his shower he threw on a pair of clean jeans and a T-shirt, then padded barefoot into the kitchen. Hannah stood at the sink shoving food down the garbage disposal. He peered over her shoulder. "That bad?"

She laughed. "That bad." She rinsed out the sink, then shut off the water and dried her hands on a towel.

He should have thought to stop somewhere for fast food on the way home. "Do you have a backup plan?"

"As a matter of fact, I do." She inched closer to him and wrapped her arms around his neck. "I thought we could feast on each other."

He grinned. "I like this plan."

She grabbed his hand and tugged him after her, hitting the light switch on the way out of the room. It took fifteen minutes to climb the stairs—too many stops to kiss and take off their clothes. By the time they tumbled onto Hannah's bed, they were naked and starving.

Hours later, Alonso stared into the darkness, holding Hannah close. He'd never felt more at peace with himself than he did at this moment, and it wasn't because he'd saved a man's life tonight. This feeling of contentment had *Hannah* written all over it, and that scared him to death.

Chapter Eight

"Looks as if I arrived just in time," Doc Snyder said when he stopped at the Blue Bison Thursday morning and caught Hannah and Alonso filling the backseat of her pickup with plastic food containers. For the past two days Hannah had been baking up a storm—all of Luke's favorite cookies. Alonso got a kick out of how excited she was to visit her brother.

"We're driving out to the boys' ranch to spend Thanksgiving Day with Luke," Hannah said. "What brings you all the way out here, Doc?"

"Thought I might have a word with Alonso."

"Did something happen to Joseph?" Alonso had called the day following Joseph's injury and Doc had assured him that there had been no complications.

"Joseph's doing fine." Doc motioned to the rockers on the porch. "Mind if I sit a spell?" He hobbled up the steps.

Hannah disappeared into the house and Alonso propped himself against the porch rail. "What can I do for you?"

"I have a favor to ask."

Alonso noticed the way Doc rubbed his thigh. "What's the matter with your leg?"

"You don't miss a thing, do you?"

"Your limp is pretty obvious."

"That's why I'm here. I've got a proposition for you."

A red flag went up inside Alonso's head, but he held his tongue.

"I've been needing hip-replacement surgery for the past three years but there's never been a good time."

Alonso dropped his gaze. *Damn.* He knew what was coming next.

"I was hoping to have the surgery after Thanksgiving, but I need someone to fill in at the clinic for me."

"I can't."

"You have a license to practice, don't you?"

"I do, but the hospital in Albuquerque needs me back by December first." He had three days left before he took off. He and Hannah hadn't discussed his impending departure but it was there in every look and every touch they shared.

He was torn about leaving. He didn't like to think of Hannah alone while Luke was at the boys' ranch. There hadn't been any more mischief but he worried about her safety. And if that wasn't enough reason to call his boss and inform him that he couldn't return just yet, then the fact that he didn't want to go was. Alonso was starting to feel revived, and he attributed his improved attitude to plenty of fresh air and physical labor even though he suspected it had more to do with Hannah.

"I'd be happy to make a call to your boss and explain the situation. Maybe he'd be willing to let you stay."

"I doubt your patients would appreciate an outsider evaluating their health."

"A person in pain doesn't care who helps them."

Couldn't Doc take no for an answer? "I'm a trauma

surgeon. I don't have experience with everyday medical ailments. You'd be better off finding a primary-care physician to take over your practice."

Doc looked disappointed but he didn't badger Alonso. He left his chair and limped down the steps. "Who's doing your surgery?" Alonso asked.

"Edward Albertson. His practice is in Albuquerque."

"Hope it goes well."

Doc grumbled something unintelligible, then got into his truck and took off.

"What did he want?" Hannah asked when she stepped outside with more cookie containers.

He rushed over to help her. "Luke is going to get sick eating all these sweets."

"He'll share them with the other boys."

Once they'd stacked the tubs in the backseat, Alonso said, "Doc needs someone to fill in for him while he recovers from his hip-replacement surgery."

Hannah's eyes lit up. "Are you going to help him?" Her excitement made Alonso feel like crap.

"I can't. I leave in three days."

Hannah forced a smile and tossed the keys to him. "You drive." She secured her seat belt. "I'm excited to see Luke. He's sounded so positive when we've talked on the phone."

For Hannah's sake, Alonso hoped Luke had turned a corner. He admired Hannah for not badgering him about his decision not to help Doc. He sensed she wanted him to stay as much as he wanted to stay but they both knew anything long-term was out of the question.

The drive to the ranch should have taken less than two hours but Hannah had needed to stop three times to use a gas-station bathroom. She'd mentioned having an upset stomach when she'd woken in the morning and had skipped breakfast, instead drinking two water bottles on the road. Alonso hoped she wasn't coming down with a virus. Then again, if she was and he caught it, he'd have a valid reason for delaying his departure another week.

When they finally arrived at the entrance to the ranch, Alonso lowered his window and pushed the security button on the gatepost. "Alonso Marquez and Hannah Buck here to see Luke Buck." The lens on the camera attached to the top of the gate swiveled toward them, then a moment later the gate swung open and he drove through.

"How can they afford all this?" Hannah pointed to the holiday plants and decorations adorning the entrance.

"Riley's family makes their money breeding Kentucky Derby horses."

"Wow."

As soon as Alonso navigated the pickup around a curve in the road, the ranch buildings came into view. "There are a lot of people here," she said.

Several vehicles sat parked in the yard and Hannah's excitement grew. As soon as they got out of the pickup, Maria appeared on the porch and waved. Hannah met her at the bottom of the steps and the women hugged. "Thank you so much for inviting us to spend the day here."

"Luke's doing great. You'll be thrilled with his attitude." Maria smiled. "I promise." She gave Alonso a hug. "Luke and the other boys are getting things ready for the rodeo this afternoon while José and the fathers are cooking the Thanksgiving dinner in the mess hall."

"Guess I better roll up my sleeves then and start peeling a few potatoes." Alonso walked off to join the men.

Maria took Hannah's hand. "The men think us ladies are baking pies in the house." She winked. "But I ordered all the pies from a bakery and had them delivered yesterday. We're playing Bunco and drinking margaritas."

Hannah laughed and followed Maria inside. "Is this the original ranch house on the property?" she asked when she entered the home and noticed the old wood floors.

"It is. Riley and I have spent a lot of money renovating the house. He wanted to tear it down and start over but I hate to destroy someone else's memories, so we added on to the structure."

They walked into a noisy kitchen with a huge farmhouse sink and plenty of counter space. "Ladies," Maria said. "This is Luke's sister. Hannah, this is Cruz Rivera's wife, Sara. Cruz and Alonso were friends in high school. Sara's father, José, is the ranch cook and Sara is a registered nurse. She runs our new health clinic."

Hannah and Sara exchanged greetings. Then Maria introduced Hannah to the mothers of the boys and wives of the ranch hands before sticking a margarita glass in her hand. "Help yourself to any of the appetizers. Dinner won't be served for a while yet." Maria held the cheese-and-cracker tray in front of Hannah and she helped herself to a cracker.

"That's all you're going to eat?"

Hannah didn't want to share that her stomach was upset, so she lied. "We stopped and grabbed a bite to eat on the way here."

Conversation resumed among the ladies and Maria

left the room to set up Bunco tables. "I'm so glad you and Alonso came today," Sara said as she helped herself to a piece of cheese. "Alonso and Cruz were best friends growing up in the barrio."

"Barrio?" How come Alonso hadn't told her that?

"Cruz always believed Alonso would make it out and do something important with his life."

"Alonso hasn't talked much about his childhood." Hannah flashed a smile. "We're just friends."

Sara's gaze made Hannah uncomfortable. It was as if the woman sensed Hannah's feelings for Alonso went deeper than friendship. "Cruz and I started out as friends, too." She smiled. "How did you two meet?"

"I almost ran over him." Sara's eyes widened and Hannah laughed. "Luke and I were arguing and I took my eyes off the road for a minute and I didn't see Alonso hitchhiking on the shoulder."

"Hitchhiking?"

"He took a leave of absence from the university hospital in Albuquerque."

"Alonso is staying at your place, then?"

"He's been helping me with ranch chores, but he has to return to the city in a few days." The end of the month was fast approaching, and Hannah tried not to think about how lonely she'd be once he left. "So how did you and Cruz meet?"

"My daughter, Dani, and I were visiting my father-in-law for the summer when Cruz walked into his restaurant in Papago Springs. Lord, he was the most handsome man I'd ever seen." She fanned her face. "At the time I was trying to convince my father-in-law to move to Albuquerque and live with me and my daughter, but he was stubborn. Then Cruz asked about the help-wanted sign in the window and I hired him to fix up the property in hopes of convincing José to put it on the market. It didn't take long for Dani or me to see that Cruz was a special man."

"Did he win over your father-in-law?"

Sara laughed. "It took José a little longer to come around." Her expression sobered. "Dani's father had passed away a few years ago, but José was still having a difficult time letting go of his son."

"I'm sorry about your husband."

"Thanks. Fortunately Cruz came into our lives at the perfect time and helped us all move on."

The love in Sara's voice when she spoke of Cruz tugged at Hannah's heartstrings. If she allowed the affection she already felt for Alonso to have free rein over her heart, it wouldn't be difficult to fall all the way in love with him.

Hannah took a sip of her margarita—a drink she normally enjoyed—but the bitter taste made her stomach churn and she set the glass on the counter.

"What's the matter?" Sara studied her face. "You're perspiring."

The urge to vomit gripped Hannah's stomach and she gasped, "Where's the bathroom?" Sara grabbed her hand and they left the kitchen. At the end of the hall she steered Hannah into a bathroom. There wasn't any time to close the door before Hannah flipped up the toilet lid and tossed her cookies.

She'd barely caught her breath before a second round of heaving hit her. Sara held Hannah's hair off her face until she finished. Then Hannah flushed the toilet and sat on the closed lid. Sara wet the end of a hand towel and mopped Hannah's face.

"I thought you looked a little green in the gills when you walked into the kitchen with Maria."

"I didn't feel well when I woke up this morning but I didn't want to cancel on Luke." Hannah stood up and cupped her hand under the water then rinsed her mouth. "I'm sorry you had to witness that."

"Have you had a flu shot?" Sara asked.

"At the beginning of October."

"What have you eaten lately?"

"Not much. I've woken up with an upset stomach the past three days. But this is the first time I've actually thrown up."

"Don't move." Sara left the bathroom then returned a minute later with a handful of soda crackers and a glass of ginger ale. "Nibble on these and take small sips of the soda."

Hannah did as instructed, surprised when the cracker stayed down. "I guess I shouldn't have gone without breakfast."

"When was the last time you had your period?"

Hannah's mouth dropped open, then she snapped it shut and shook her head. "I'm not pregnant."

"You're sure?"

"Positive." She couldn't be pregnant. She and Alonso always used a condom when they had sex.

Except the first two times.

Hannah counted back the days since she'd picked up Alonso on the side of the road—twenty-six. And she should have had her period last week. So she was a little late. There was a first time for everything. Besides, all the stress she was under was probably messing with her body.

"If you don't feel better in a week, you should see a doctor."

"I will."

"I'd take it easy on the food today," Sara said.

Hannah nodded. Right now, none of the traditional Thanksgiving foods appealed to her.

Sara escorted Hannah into the front parlor. "Sit here for a while and rest. I'll tell Maria you're passing on the first few rounds of Bunco."

"Thanks, Sara." After the nurse left, Hannah closed her eyes. She refused to consider the possibility that she was pregnant with Alonso's baby. Clinging to that stubborn thought, she drifted off.

"C'mon, sleepyhead, we're ready to carry the pies to the bunkhouse and start our Thanksgiving celebration."

Hannah woke with a start and popped off the couch. She rubbed her eyes until Maria came into focus. "I'm sorry. How long have I been sleeping?"

"Not long." Maria's gaze dropped to Hannah's stomach. "The other ladies left already."

Hannah followed Maria out of the house, hoping the older woman wouldn't mention her getting sick to anyone—specifically Alonso. When they entered the dining hall Luke surprised her with a bear hug.

"Wait until you taste José's food, Hannah." He led her to the chow line that consisted of two picnic tables covered with food. She spotted Alonso talking with Sara's husband, and when he noticed her his gaze warmed. Despite still feeling a little nauseous, his stare made her heart beat faster.

She and Luke filled their plates then sat at a table for four in the corner. A few minutes later Alonso joined them. Then Maria walked to the front of the room and

We'd like to send you two free books like the one you are enjoying now. Your two books have a combined price of over $10, but they are yours to keep absolutely FREE! We'll even send you 2 wonderful surprise gifts. You can't lose!

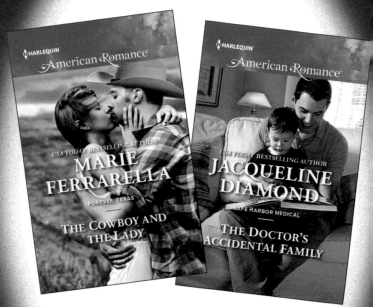

REMEMBER: Your Free Merchandise, consisting of **2 Free Books** and **2 Free Gifts**, is worth over $20.00! No purchase is necessary, so please send for your Free Merchandise today.

Get TWO FREE GIFTS!

We'll also send you two wonderful FREE GIFTS (worth about $10), in addition to your 2 Free books!

Visit us at:
www.ReaderService.com

YOUR FREE MERCHANDISE INCLUDES...
2 FREE Books **AND** 2 FREE Mystery Gifts

FREE MERCHANDISE VOUCHER

2 FREE
BOOKS
and
2 FREE
GIFTS

Please send my Free Merchandise, consisting of
2 Free Books and **2 Free Mystery Gifts**.
I understand that I am under no obligation to buy
anything, as explained on the back of this card.

154/354 HDL GJAH

Please Print

FIRST NAME

LAST NAME

ADDRESS

APT.#   CITY

STATE/PROV.   ZIP/POSTAL CODE

NO PURCHASE NECESSARY!

AR-N15-FM15

BUSINESS REPLY MAIL
FIRST-CLASS MAIL   PERMIT NO. 717   BUFFALO, NY

POSTAGE WILL BE PAID BY ADDRESSEE

READER SERVICE
PO BOX 1867
BUFFALO NY 14240-9952

NO POSTAGE
NECESSARY
IF MAILED
IN THE
UNITED STATES

◀ If offer card is missing write to: Reader Service, P.O. Box 1867, Buffalo, NY 14240-1867 or visit www.ReaderService.com ▶

Alonso chuckled.

"What?"

"Your mouth is open."

"He never takes his dishes to the sink at home. This place is magical."

Luke handed Alonso a plate with a huge slice of pumpkin pie on it then sat down and ate his own dessert. "I can't wait to show you how I mark out. I've been working on it all week."

"What's mark out?" Hannah asked.

"Rolling your spurs along the horse's neck." Luke smiled. "It's not easy when the bronc is trying to buck you off."

"How's your schoolwork going?" Hannah asked.

"The same. I'm getting Bs on everything."

"That's great." She nudged his side. "Does Maria have to twist your arm to make you do your homework?"

"No." He glanced around the room.

Hannah suspected he was itching to go off with his friends. "Has there been any trouble between the boys?"

"Everybody here is cool. But this one kid—" Luke lowered his voice "—almost got kicked out."

"Why?"

"Michael ran away and Mr. Fitzgerald spent all day tracking him down."

"Why'd he run?" All sorts of things came to Hannah's mind—too much homework, other boys teasing him, having too many chores to do.

"A social worker had showed up and told Mr. Fitzgerald that they had a spot for Michael in a group home, but Michael said he'd been in one of those places before and he was never gonna go back."

Poor kid.

"Mr. Fitzgerald's gonna work it out so Michael can stay here until he's eighteen."

"That's nice of Mr. Fitzgerald." Hannah's gaze connected with Alonso's. Things might have turned out differently for Luke if they hadn't come upon Alonso walking along the highway a few weeks ago.

"I wouldn't mind staying here until I turned eighteen," Luke said.

"Hey, no way," Hannah said, feeling a little hurt that he was okay living away from her. "I need your help running the ranch."

"I know." The excitement in Luke's eyes dimmed.

Hannah searched for something to say that would bring the smile back to her brother's face, but nothing came to mind. Thankfully Cruz Rivera walked to the front of the room and clanged a spoon against the side of a drinking glass. The crowd quieted. "We have a special treat for all of our guests this afternoon. The boys have been working real hard on their rodeo skills and they'd like to show you what they've learned," he said.

A little girl tugged on his jeans. "What about me, Daddy?"

Cruz smiled. "Excuse me, the boys and girl have worked extra hard." He chuckled. "First up is our mutton bustin' competition. All the little kids are welcome to give it a try. Let's head out to the corral and have some fun."

"See you out there." Luke took off with a group of boys.

"Good luck!" Hannah shouted after him.

The dining hall emptied out and Hannah walked with Alonso to the corral, eager to escape the food smells that had played havoc with her stomach the past hour.

"Did you ever do any mutton bustin' when you were little?" he asked.

"Twice. I was six or seven. If I remember correctly, I fell off pretty quick, but it was fun."

The parents with young children inched closer to the corral, where Cruz and Riley helped the kids put on a protective helmet and a padded vest. Hannah nodded to the metal bleachers. "I'm going to grab a seat."

"Mind if I stay here where the action is?" Alonso squeezed her hand.

"Go ahead." Hannah sat by herself away from the perfume smells of the other women. She enjoyed watching the kids squeal and laugh when they fell off the sheep. Before her father died, Hannah had envisioned herself one day marrying and having a few kids. Her hand automatically went to her stomach. She couldn't be pregnant. Not now. She shoved the thought to the back of her mind and focused on the activity in the corral. She had enough worries; she didn't need to add one more to the list.

After the mutton bustin' contest ended, the older kids lined up for the bronc bustin'. Alonso and Riley encouraged the boys and Cruz coached them through their rides.

Most of the teens ended up in the dirt but a few managed to ride for more than three seconds. Then it was Luke's turn. When he waved to her, she stuck her fingers inside her mouth and let loose a shrill whistle.

Luke lowered himself onto the back of the bronc, and Hannah expected him to fuss with the rope. Instead, he took no time to prepare before nodding to the gateman. The chute opened and the bronc lunged into the arena, throwing Luke's upper body over the horse's head. Luke managed to hold on as the horse spun.

Time slowed to a crawl and just when she thought he'd make it to the buzzer, Luke slid sideways and dropped to the ground. She held her breath, waiting for him to roll away from the horse's hooves, and not until he stood up and ran to the chute did she exhale in relief.

Luke and Alonso exchanged high fives with Cruz, and her brother's goofy grin brought tears to Hannah's eyes. She hadn't seen him this excited since before their father had passed away. Riding broncs made Luke happy, and she hoped that his dream of rodeoing would keep him in school and out of trouble.

After the final ride of the afternoon Riley and Maria thanked everyone for spending the day with them, then the parents began saying their goodbyes. Luke walked her and Alonso back to the pickup so he could get his cookies.

"Thanks for coming," he said.

Hannah hugged him. "I'm glad you're doing well, but I miss you."

Luke laughed. "No, you don't."

She handed him the plastic containers. "They're all your favorites."

"Jeez, Hannah. Did you make, like, five hundred dozen?"

"Just about." She punched his arm playfully. "I'll see you right before Christmas." Only four more weeks until Luke came home for good.

"Keep studying," Alonso said.

"I will."

Hannah couldn't delay the goodbye any longer. "Talk to you next week sometime."

"Okay."

Alonso started the engine and Hannah waved as they drove away. Luke didn't even glance over his shoulder after he walked off.

When Alonso turned onto the highway, he said, "You're awfully quiet."

"I don't think he missed me."

"He missed you, just not as much as you'd hoped, maybe."

"I'm glad he's having a good time." And she meant it. "I'm tired. Making all those cookies was a lot of work."

"Go to sleep. I'll listen to music."

Hannah leaned her head against the window, closed her eyes and tried not to think about what Sara had asked her in the bathroom earlier that day. Hannah didn't know how much time had passed when Alonso shook her shoulder and woke her.

"I've got to gas up. Wasn't sure if you needed to use the bathroom or not."

"Thanks." Hannah went into the store, used the restroom, then browsed the feminine supplies. *Bingo*. She paid for a pregnancy test kit and a bag of black licorice, then returned to the truck, where Alonso waited.

He nodded to the paper bag. "What did you buy?"

She took out the licorice, careful to conceal the other item from his view. "Want one?"

"No, thanks."

She ate a few pieces then stowed the bag on the floor by her feet and dozed off again. The next time she opened her eyes they were home.

"I'll check on Buster," he said.

Hannah hurried into the house and went straight upstairs to the bathroom, where she locked the door, then sat on the edge of the tub and read the test kit instructions. She followed the directions, then decided to take a shower while she waited for the results. Once she dried off and slipped into her pj's she turned over the stick.

PREGNANT.

It couldn't get any clearer than that. She shoved the stick into the box and the box into the paper bag and the bag into her makeup drawer. Too stunned to process the news, she went into her room and crawled beneath the bedcovers. A few minutes later she heard the shower in Luke's room turn on.

Not long after, Alonso whispered her name when he crawled into her bed and snuggled against her. His warm, naked body pressed into her backside. He slid an arm beneath her pillow and one around her belly—where their baby rested inside her.

This couldn't be happening. To her. *To them.*

Alonso had another life waiting for him in Albuquerque, and her future was right here on the ranch. She turned in his arms and pressed her mouth to his. Whenever Alonso held her, she forgot all her troubles.

Tomorrow morning she'd tell him they were about to become parents, but tonight she wanted to pretend it was just the two of them.

Chapter Nine

Startled awake, Hannah stared wide-eyed at the ceiling, her brain registering a sharp pain in her face. Before she understood what had happened, something smacked her in the head and she jumped inside her skin.

"Stop him!"

Alonso's shout cleared Hannah's foggy brain and she rolled to the opposite side of the mattress. She pressed her fingers to her throbbing cheek and watched helplessly as Alonso's arms flailed in the air.

"He's wearing a bomb!"

Dear God. Her own pain forgotten, she attempted to shake him awake, but he was too strong and pulled away. She sprang from the bed and turned on the light. "Wake up, Alonso!"

"Get down!" He flew off the bed, grabbed her around the waist and threw her to the floor, landing on top of her with his full body weight. The air whooshed from her lungs, and she gasped for breath. Tears of pain filled her eyes and she shoved hard against his chest, "Get off me!"

"Hang on, Tony! Damn it, buddy, hang on!" Alonso squeezed Hannah so hard she couldn't draw a breath.

"Nooo!"

The pain in Alonso's voice brought new tears to her eyes. She hated to hurt him, but he might injure her worse if he didn't wake up from his nightmare. She rammed her knee into his crotch and he released her, then rolled onto his back and moaned.

Hannah scrambled to her feet and grabbed her bathrobe off the back of the bedroom door, then ran downstairs to the kitchen and poured herself a glass of orange juice. Her hands shook as she drank the juice. Once she finished, she poured a glass for Alonso, intending to take it up to him, but she found him sitting at the bottom of the stairs, his bare chest glistening with sweat.

She handed him the drink.

"Hannah." He set the glass on the step and caressed her face. "Did I hurt you?"

Her nose felt a little numb, but she shook her head. "I'm okay."

"Your eye is starting to bruise." He gently pressed his fingers against her cheekbones and nose. "Nothing feels broken." He threaded his fingers through her hair and felt her scalp, then cursed. "You have a bump back here."

"My head clunked against the floor when you fell on top of me."

He took her by the hand and led her to the kitchen, then made her sit at the table. He rummaged through the freezer and pulled out a bag of frozen corn, wrapped it in a dish towel, then sat next to her and held it against the bump. "I'm sorry."

"It's okay. I know you didn't mean to hurt me."

"No, it's not okay." He bowed his head.

"Tell me about it," she said.

"Tell you about what?"

"The nightmare. You shouted something about a bomb."

She watched the struggle in his eyes before he placed her hand on the bag of corn, then stood at the sink with his back to her. "I haven't had that nightmare since I returned to the States."

If it was that painful to talk about she shouldn't make him. "Never mind. You don't have to tell me."

"It was Wednesday. Earlier that morning a Humvee from the base went out to deliver supplies to a village and drove over a roadside bomb. Three of the soldiers suffered severe injuries. I spent hours in surgery, but I saved their lives." He paced between the stove and the fridge. "They were still in recovery when an Afghan medic I was training walked into the recovery room, wearing a bomb strapped to his chest."

"How did you escape injury?"

"I dived through a door into a hallway, but the soldiers I'd just saved were lying in their beds and…"

Hannah pictured the gruesome scene in her head. "I'm so sorry you lost your friends." He didn't say anything. "You called out Tony's name."

"Tony was my best friend. He'd just found out the day before that his wife had given birth to a son." Alonso closed his eyes. "The Humvee accident blew off his leg, but he'd begged me to save him so he could go home and see his son." Alonso smacked his fist against the fridge. "I saved him, but for what? So he could get blown up all over again?"

Hannah's stomach grew queasy.

"You look as if you're going to faint," Alonso said.

She set the bag of corn on the table and took slow, easy breaths, hoping the morning sickness would pass.

Until just now, she'd forgotten about being pregnant. She closed her eyes, willing the tears to go away. Tears of frustration and fear.

Fear of being a mother when she wasn't ready to be one. Fear of assuming more responsibility when she was already up to her eyeballs in running the ranch and making sure her brother toed the line.

And then there was Alonso. He was leaving in three days and she was afraid he'd feel obligated to stick around longer because of the baby—not her.

You knew before you slept with him that nothing permanent would come of your relationship.

But that was before she'd got pregnant.

The tears trapped beneath her eyelids leaked out and slid down her cheeks. Alonso knelt on the floor by her chair and held her hands. "God, Hannah, I'm sorry I hurt you." His tortured gaze held her captive. "I'll help with the chores this morning, then pack my things and hit the road." He pressed a finger against her mouth when she tried to speak. "I had to leave Sunday anyway to report in at the hospital."

Her heart broke. His earnest expression betrayed how eager he was to leave. "I have something to tell you."

"What?"

She hesitated, knowing the next two words would change his life forever. "I'm pregnant."

Alonso released Hannah's hands and sprang to his feet, then backpedaled until he hit the wall. He stared at her as if he was seeing a ghost.

The word *pregnant* reverberated inside Alonso's head until he thought he'd go deaf. He opened his mouth to speak, but couldn't draw any air into his lungs.

"I think it happened the first time we…"

Of course it had happened then, because he'd made sure he'd used a condom after that night. The nightmare and the shock of discovering that he'd hurt Hannah, and now learning that he was going to be a father...

He couldn't breathe. He lunged for the back door and stumbled out to the porch. The lungful of cold air he sucked in only added to the numbness in his brain. He couldn't think right now and nothing made sense.

He went back into the house, walked right past Hannah without making eye contact, then went into Luke's room and finished dressing. He grabbed the keys to the Civic off the table in the hallway and returned into the kitchen.

"Tell me it's going to be okay." Hannah's whisper reached him before he made it to the door.

"I can't, Hannah. I can't guarantee anything will ever be okay." He closed the door, then hopped into the Civic and sped off, the car bouncing like a rubber ball on the gravel road. When he reached the highway, he turned toward Paradise. He resisted the temptation to stop at Maloney's on the way into town—getting drunk wouldn't make Hannah's pregnancy go away.

A baby. He couldn't wrap his mind around it. He'd never considered becoming a father. Had never been in a relationship long enough with one woman for the subject to even come up.

It was almost 7:00 a.m. when he arrived in town. Nothing but the gas station convenience store was open. He pulled into the parking lot. The blurry-eyed clerk managed a "good morning" when Alonso entered the store. He filled a large foam cup with black coffee, then studied the day-old doughnuts before selecting a package of Twinkies.

Back in the car Alonso choked down the sweet cake. The hit of sugar released his anger and he slammed his fist against the dashboard. The situation he found himself in was no one's fault but his own. He should have kept walking the day Hannah had almost run him off the road. But her sweet smile and pretty blue eyes had sucked him in and now he was paying the price.

A heavy price.

He wasn't ready to be a father. Hell, he'd never planned on having kids.

He'd seen too much during his lifetime—the world chewed up and spit out the innocent.

Maybe Hannah doesn't want to keep the baby.

He hadn't stuck around to ask how she felt about the situation. Shoot, her life was as complicated as his, and raising a child would add to her to-do list every day. And if Luke returned to the ranch at Christmas and reverted to his old ways and didn't help Hannah, then she'd be in a world of hurt.

He drove back to the ranch. Only an hour had passed since he'd left, but when he entered the kitchen Hannah was still sitting at the table, a vacant expression on her face. He felt like crap for running out the way he had. "I'm going to feed the bison."

"You don't have to do that. I know you want to leave."

"I'll stay until you decide what you want to do about the baby."

Her eyes widened. "I'm keeping it."

"You might change your mind." Right now the baby didn't seem real to him.

She got up from the chair and took a box of cornflakes off the pantry shelf. "You don't have to stay, Alonso."

"I'm fifty percent to blame."

She poured a small amount of cereal into a bowl. "I'm not getting an abortion."

"This is a big decision, Hannah. A child is a life-long responsibility." He ought to know. His mother had struggled to keep food on the table and a roof over her kids' heads.

"I helped raise Luke. I realize how much work a baby's going to be." She shoved a spoonful of cornflakes into her mouth and a drop of milk dripped off her chin.

"I don't know if I can always be there for you." There, he'd said it. Put it out in the open instead of beating around the bush.

"I don't expect anything from you."

She damn well should. "You can count on me for financial support." *But anything else...*

She finished her cereal, then set the bowl in the sink and faced him. "I don't think you should stay."

She's giving you an out—take it.

He ignored his conscience. "I don't feel good about leaving you alone when the sheriff hasn't caught those responsible for vandalizing the ranch."

The steely look in Hannah's eyes insisted he wouldn't change her mind. "I'll feed the bison this morning."

"I said I would."

"And I said I don't want you to."

"Hannah."

"What?"

He wanted to tell her that she could try to push him away all she wanted but he wasn't leaving until they discussed the future—more specifically what role she wanted him to play in their child's life. "Mind if I use

Luke's car?" He felt stupid for asking when he'd taken off in the Civic a short while ago.

"I don't care what you do."

Alonso read the truth in her eyes—she didn't care whether he stayed or left. She'd given him his walking papers, so why did that make him angry?

HANNAH STOOD IN the shadows inside the barn and watched Alonso drive off in the Civic.

I'm going to be okay.

If she repeated the phrase a thousand times over, she might start believing it. Fat chance, when she'd never felt this scared or desperate before. Not even when her mother had walked out years ago and left her behind had she been as frightened when she imagined the future.

Hannah was grateful that Alonso had loaded the hay for the bison before they'd left for the boys' ranch yesterday. She backed the truck up to the trailer and secured the hitch, then drove out to find the herd. The bumpy ride upset her stomach, so she slowed down and tried to make sense of all the thoughts clamoring inside her head.

What kind of a life would this baby have without a stable family?

Hannah had panicked after Alonso had insisted he'd stay—she didn't want to be his responsibility. Even though she'd loved her father and Luke, she understood how tiresome it was to take care of others. Alonso didn't love her, yet he wanted to do right by her. She couldn't do that to him.

Not even for the baby's sake?

Her vision blurred and she cursed. Darn it, she hadn't cried this much in the past five years. He'd promised financial support, but would that be enough? The idea of Alonso not being involved in their child's life didn't sit well with Hannah. She'd grown up believing her mother hadn't loved her. No child should have to live with being abandoned by a parent.

"Oh, no." Hannah hit the brake. The section of fence they'd repaired a short time ago was torn down again. Thank goodness the bison were in the north pasture on the other side of the property. At least she wouldn't have to apologize to the Markhams and ask for help retrieving her animals from their land.

She phoned Sheriff Miller and left a voice mail then drove a half mile until the herd came into view. After dropping the hay from the trailer bed she returned to the house, made herself a cup of tea and sat in the rocker on the porch to wait for the sheriff.

An hour later a plume of dust appeared. The sheriff led a smaller vehicle toward the house. As they drew closer she recognized the Civic. Alonso was back.

The concerned look on Alonso's face tugged at her heartstrings. The poor man had his share of problems—he didn't need to be saddled with hers.

The sheriff stopped the patrol car near the porch and lowered the passenger-side window. "I'll drive out and take a look at the fence. Maybe I'll get lucky and find evidence left behind."

After the sheriff drove off, Alonso spoke. "Are you okay?"

"I'm fine."

"I'll get the fencing wire from the barn and an extra pair of gloves." Halfway to the barn he stopped, then returned to the porch. "If you're not feeling well I can see if Seth Markham will help me repair the fence."

"I'm fine." She had to be fine—what other choice did she have? "And I meant what I said. You don't have to stay."

"And I meant what I said. I'm staying."

But for how long?

"Hannah."

"What?"

"You'll let me know before you decide anything about the baby?"

"I told you, I'm keeping it."

"I know, but I thought you might feel differently knowing I won't be there to help you."

"I won't change my mind." Whether Alonso helped her or not, motherhood still scared her senseless.

Alonso studied her, his brown eyes filling with concern. "Neither one of us is ready for this, but I'm glad you're keeping the baby."

Relief filled her. If he was glad, then maybe after he got used to the idea of being a father, he'd change his mind about wanting to be involved in their child's life.

"You haven't seen a doctor."

Hannah jumped and Alonso regretted startling her. She sat at the desk in the living room, balancing her checkbook and looking sexier than a woman had a right to in jeans and an oversize sweatshirt. She'd been edgy ever since she'd told him about the baby two weeks ago.

To be fair, so had he—ever since he'd informed his boss at the hospital that he wouldn't be returning to the ER until after the first of the year. His boss hadn't been pleased with the news and had told Alonso that if he didn't show up in January he'd no longer have a job. With the baby coming, Hannah knew he was concerned about being fired.

"You're about seven weeks along. You should have a blood test to check your iron levels." And other screens.

She swiveled on the chair and stared at him. "I'll make an appointment."

"With Doc Snyder?"

She shook her head. "I don't want anyone finding out before I tell Luke."

"Are you hungry?"

She glanced at the wall clock. "A little."

"I'll fix supper tonight." Alonso disappeared into the kitchen and washed up at the sink. A short time later he heard the steps creaking on the staircase, then the bathroom door opening and closing.

There wasn't much in the fridge, but he found a pound of hamburger in the freezer, a bag of noodles and cans of crushed tomatoes in the pantry. He'd make spaghetti. Once he threw all the ingredients for the sauce together, he let it simmer, then he filled a pot with water and set it to boil. By the time he dumped the cooked spaghetti noodles into a colander, an hour had passed.

He went into the front hall and glanced up the staircase. The bathroom door next to the landing stood open. Hannah had finished showering. Maybe she'd fallen asleep in her room. He climbed the stairs and peeked past the partially open door, then almost swallowed his tongue.

Wet hair plastered against her back, Hannah stood naked before the dresser mirror, examining her still-flat belly from different angles. A few more weeks and she'd develop a baby bump. He shifted his gaze to her breasts—those definitely appeared larger. He could have stared at her for hours, but he backed away, not wanting to interrupt the private moment. He tiptoed down to the first floor, then yelled, "Supper's ready!"

"Be right there!"

Back in the kitchen he grabbed a handful of ice cubes from the freezer and pressed them against his forehead, hoping the cold would erase the image of Hannah's naked body from his memory.

"Do you have a headache?" She stood in the doorway, wearing flannel pj's and a bathrobe.

He tossed the ice into the sink and wiped his face on a paper towel. "What can I get you to drink?" he asked, ignoring her question.

"I'll stick with water." Once Alonso served up the spaghetti and sat across from her, she said, "According to Maria, Luke completed all his class work for this semester."

"That's great. He didn't fall behind." He caught her playing with her food. "What's the matter? You don't like my spaghetti?"

"It's fine." She flashed a smile. "Thanks for making it."

"Why the frown?"

"I'm worried Luke will get into trouble over the winter break."

"I'd offer to stay past Christmas, but if I don't report back to the hospital before the first of the year, I won't have a job." Now that he had a child to provide for, he had to bring in a paycheck.

"Maria and Riley are taking a group of boys to compete in a junior rodeo this weekend. We're invited."

"Where's the rodeo?"

"Los Alamos. I'd like to see Luke."

"Then, we'll go." He twirled the noodles with his fork. "Is Cruz going to be there?"

"Maria didn't say." She sipped her water. "I'll be glad to have Luke back, but I worry that he won't be able to make new friends at school next semester."

"The other kids will notice that he's changed for the better. Don't worry…he'll be fine." Alonso switched the subject. "What about you? You grew up on this ranch. Did you have many friends?"

"I had several friends until high school."

"What happened to them?"

"My father's drinking grew worse and I didn't have time to socialize, because I had to take on more and more responsibility around the ranch. I missed most of the football games and the parties. Eventually my girlfriends quit calling me."

Alonso had made it all the way through high school with two good friends. Actually, they'd been more like brothers. Then Cruz had landed in jail and Vic had gone off the grid for a while. Maria had been so upset over Cruz's situation that she'd focused on Alonso, insisting he go to college. He'd wanted to escape the barrio so he'd allowed Maria to guide him through the college admission process.

"Did Luke play any football?" he asked.

"No, but my father played in high school. He received a scholarship offer from the University of New Mexico."

"He played for the Lobos?"

"No. My grandfather guilted him into staying here and helping him."

"That's too bad."

"Dad didn't talk about the past, but I'm guessing his

troubled relationship with my grandfather was one of the reasons he drank."

"Do you think he was happy managing the ranch?"

"I think he wanted to run it into the ground."

It must have been difficult for Hannah to watch her father neglect the property. Alonso's father was no winner but at least he hadn't been around to make his life miserable.

"I can't remember how many times I told my father that I loved this ranch and I'd take good care of it after he wasn't here anymore."

"What did he say?"

"That I should move to the city and find a man to marry."

Ouch. The man sounded as if he didn't care about his daughter's happiness. "Was your father close to Luke?"

"Not really. Luke looks like his mother and reminded my father of Ruth's infidelity."

Alonso finished his meal in silence. Hannah's father had let her down in the worst way. Then Seth had hurt her when he'd only proposed in hopes of joining their ranches. Luke was all Hannah had left, and he was a handful.

And then Alonso had got her pregnant. He was in the profession of saving lives, not ruining them, so why did he feel as if his baby wasn't a blessing but just another responsibility Hannah had to take on?

Chapter Ten

"Hannah? Are you ready?"

"Coming!"

Hannah crawled to her feet and flushed the toilet, then gargled with mouthwash. She hoped her morning sickness would go away so she could make it to the rodeo in Los Alamos without having to ask Alonso to pull off the road. Every morning she was reminded that she carried a baby, and she waited with anticipation for that first feeling of joy to overcome her, but so far nothing. She blamed it on the uncertainty that shrouded her relationship with Alonso.

"You want me to drive?" he asked when she stepped onto the porch.

She held out the keys. "That would be great, thanks." He opened the truck door for her and she noticed his frown.

"What's the matter?"

"Nothing, why?"

"You look miffed."

"I'm fine." He shifted into Drive, then turned on the radio.

He was mad.

She yawned. Her morning date with the toilet had

exhausted her. "I hope being away from home improved Luke's attitude about ranch chores." As her pregnancy advanced she'd need his help even more, and she worried that he would grow to resent the baby.

"Try to keep your expectations in check."

"Are you speaking from your experience at the Gateway Ranch?"

"You remembered the name."

She paid attention to everything Alonso said, because she cared about him. More than was good for her heart. "Your time there didn't turn you around immediately?"

"It did and it didn't. I was a different person at the ranch. When I went home to the barrio, I reverted to the old Alonso so I wouldn't get beat up."

"Luke's lost several friends since our father died. If he stays out of trouble, I'm hoping he'll win some of them back." A lull in conversation ensued and Hannah searched for a new topic. He hadn't mentioned the baby since he'd asked if she'd scheduled a doctor's appointment. "Have you been thinking about baby names?" He glanced at her, eyes wide with surprise. "What?" she asked. "Did you not think I'd let you have a say in naming our baby?"

He shrugged, but didn't offer any suggestions. Maybe he didn't care.

"I made an appointment for next week with a doctor in Albuquerque."

"Good."

"Don't mention it to Luke." When he frowned, she said, "I know what you're thinking."

"You do?"

"You think because I want to keep my pregnancy a secret that I'm still not sure about keeping the baby."

When he didn't protest, she knew she'd guessed right. "I'm keeping the baby."

His hands tightened on the wheel and his mouth flattened into a firm line. When he didn't immediately respond, Hannah's stomach grew queasy for a second time that morning. "Is it that you don't want to be a father or you don't want to be the father of my baby?"

"It's not that… It's…"

"What?" Why couldn't he just spit it out?

"I've experienced a lot of bad in this world. I grew up around gangs. I've seen what human beings are capable of doing to each other and it's not a good place to raise a child."

Hannah took comfort in learning that it wasn't her being the mother of his child that worried him. She didn't want to make light of Alonso's childhood or the struggles he'd faced growing up in a large city. And after losing his friends in Afghanistan, she couldn't blame him for believing the world was a crappy place.

"There's still plenty of good and kindness out there." Good grief, he was an example of that—he'd saved Joseph's life. And he was helping her with the ranch while Luke was away. "I haven't seen all the bad you have. Maybe that's the beauty of living a rural life. We see and hear about all the bad in the world on TV but we're mostly removed from it."

"Hannah, you're not removed from it. There's an ugly side of Paradise if you care to look closely."

She opened her mouth to defend her town, then snapped it shut. Her neighbor had tried to take advantage of her. Someone was destroying her property. And two delinquents had held up the convenience store.

Okay, so the town of Paradise wasn't a true paradise, but it wasn't a horrible place to live, either.

"If you're tired of city life why don't you move to a smaller town?" *Somewhere closer to Paradise.*

"There aren't many positions for trauma surgeons in smaller hospitals."

Hannah couldn't picture herself living anywhere but the ranch, and Alonso's future would always be in a large hospital where he could help the most people. She'd better wrap her head around the idea that he might only see her and the baby once in a while. Other than a check in the mail every month, she couldn't count on him to help her raise their child.

Alonso switched lanes and took the exit off the highway. Two stoplights later he turned right and a half mile down the road he pulled into the fairgrounds.

"Looks like a big crowd today." He handed the attendant a five-dollar bill, then followed the line of vehicles and parked in the next available space.

"Did Maria say when the boys would arrive?"

"The rodeo starts at one." He hopped out, then came over to her side of the truck and held the door open for her. "They should be here soon." He took her hand and they walked to the entrance. "We have time to kill. Let's check out the livestock barns."

The warmth of Alonso's touch cajoled Hannah into forgetting her worries—at least for now. Time passed quickly as he talked about rodeo and bucking horses. She half listened to his spiel, her focus falling by the wayside when he placed his hand against her back or touched her shoulder. She could get used to this man being in her life every day.

"Hannah!" Luke jogged toward them. Hannah tugged her hand free from Alonso's grip and hugged her brother.

"You look like a real cowboy in that getup," she said.

Luke shook Alonso's hand. "Glad you guys are here. My ride's at one thirty."

"Saddle bronc?" Alonso asked.

Luke nodded. "I drew Midnight Express."

Hannah squeezed his arm. "Are you sure you're ready?"

"Cruz said I'm ready."

"Where is Cruz?" Alonso asked.

"He's not here. He said he didn't want all the attention on him and that we shouldn't let any gossip we hear distract us."

"Did Mr. Fitzgerald come with you?"

"Nope."

Hannah shot Alonso a worried glance.

"Sweet Pete drove the van here." Luke pointed to the older cowboy standing with the other teens. "Cruz said we're supposed to find Victor Vicario. He's competing today and Cruz said he might give us some pointers."

Alonso scanned the crowd but didn't see anyone who resembled his friend.

"Vicario's riding first to help raise money for an inner-city kids' club in Albuquerque. He's doing it as a favor to Mr. Fitzgerald."

Alonso nodded to the stands filling up. "Now I understand why there's a big crowd here."

"And Cruz said Vicario's holding a clinic after the rodeo for any junior cowboys who want pointers. Sweet Pete said we could stay for it."

"How many boys are competing this afternoon?" Hannah asked.

"There's five of us."

"You two visit for a while," Alonso said. "I'll see if I can find Vic."

That Victor had volunteered to ride in a fund-raiser surprised Alonso. Back in high school, his friend had only been interested in making a quick buck for himself. Keeping his eyes peeled for his buddy, Alonso cut across the grounds and made his way to the bucking chutes. The area was crammed with young cowboys and their families.

"You looking for me?"

Alonso pulled up short when Victor cut him off. "Hell, yes, I'm looking for you." He grasped Vic's shoulder and gave him a bro hug. "It's been a few years. You look good."

Vic scowled and Alonso regretted his comment. His friend had always been self-conscious of the thick scar that marred his face. "You have time to talk?" he asked.

"My ride's parked outside." Vic led the way to a smaller lot behind the arena, then dropped the tailgate on his truck and the two men hopped up.

"It's been a long time, Vic."

"You don't have to tell me how many years have passed since…"

Cruz landed in prison.

"I'm surprised you're riding the circuit." Alonso chuckled. "Last I knew you said it hurt your ass too much to fall off a bronc."

Vic returned Alonso's grin, the gesture stretching the scar, which tugged one side of his mouth down. The mark wasn't pretty, and time had only made it more prominent because Vic had lost all his baby fat, leaving his face lean and chiseled. When they'd hung out together in the 'hood, girls would approach them, but as soon as they saw Vic's face up close, they'd cringe and walk the other way.

"Stuff happens and plans change. Maria said you left the Army."

"How often do you talk to her?"

"Once a month. She's always checking up on me."

"We're lucky that she cares about us."

"So what happened with your Army career?"

"Like you said, stuff happens. It was time to get out. I'm a trauma surgeon at the university hospital in Albuquerque."

"What are you doing down this way?"

"I took some time off from the job."

"Why?"

For a guy who didn't discuss his own life, Vic liked to poke his nose in Alonso's business. "I needed a break. That's all."

"Maria says I'm supposed to take a look at this Luke Buck kid and give him a few pointers. She said you're sweet on his sister." Vic grinned.

"Luke and Hannah's parents are gone and it's just the two of them on their ranch now. They raise bison for specialty meat markets. I've been helping her with chores since Luke went to the boys' ranch."

"How'd you end up meeting them?"

"Hitchhiking."

"Are you and Hannah a couple?"

Not in the way Vic was asking. "We're just friends." *Who are expecting a baby together.*

Alonso nudged Vic's arm. "How about you? You got a wife or girlfriend?"

He shook his head. "Too busy traveling the circuit."

"I don't keep up with rodeo. I found out through Maria that Cruz broke all the rodeo records at White Sands."

"If he hadn't gone to prison he would have won a national title," Vic said.

"Maybe. He seems pretty happy working with the boys at Maria and Riley's ranch."

"That wasn't his destiny."

"Like you riding the circuit now wasn't your destiny?" When Vic didn't answer, Alonso asked, "How long you gonna keep at it?"

Vic slid off the tailgate. "Until I win a national title." He adjusted his Stetson. "I better head back to the chutes and check on the boys." He held out his hand. "Good luck with your job."

Alonso would need more than luck to get out of the situation he found himself in with Hannah.

"I CAN'T BELIEVE you're coming home in another week," Hannah said after she and Luke sat down at a table near the concession stand.

"I kinda wish I didn't have to go back to school next semester."

"It won't be so bad."

"I've made new friends at the ranch." Luke's eyes strayed to the teens signing in at the event table near the entrance.

"Luke." When he didn't acknowledge her, she spoke louder. "Luke."

"Huh?"

"Am I the reason you don't want to come home?" They'd always been close until their father had passed away.

"It's not you. It's just that I hate ranch work. I can do what I want here in my free time. Like learn rodeo."

"I realize you don't love ranching the way I do and I promise I won't stand in your way after you graduate from high school. If you want to leave and go rodeo you can."

"But who's going to help you? You can't stay there by yourself."

She laughed. "Why not? A woman can manage a ranch just as well as a man." *If not better.*

"What if something happens to you? There won't be anyone to call for help."

"We have neighbors, Luke, and I carry a cell phone." She punched him playfully in the shoulder. "And Dad taught us both how to shoot a rifle. I'll use it if I have to."

Her brother didn't look convinced. "If I rodeo I'm going to need money."

Hannah swallowed a sigh. "Maybe I can buy your share of the ranch."

He sat up straighter. "What do you mean?"

She waved her hand. "If rodeo is what you want to do, then I can apply for a bank loan to buy your half of the ranch. You could use the money for a new pickup and to help finance your rodeo career until you start winning."

"You'd do that for me?"

"As long as you graduate from high school I'm willing to do whatever it takes to help you succeed." *Even if I go into debt the rest of my life.*

"You should've married Seth. Then you wouldn't have to be alone."

Hannah pressed her hand against her stomach. Little did Luke know she wouldn't be alone for long. "Hey, don't worry about me. I'll be fine."

Luke dropped the subject and asked, "Has there been any more trouble on the ranch?"

"We had an incident," she said. "Someone broke another section of the fence."

Luke dropped his gaze. Maybe he felt guilty that he was enjoying his time at the boys' ranch while she had to deal with expensive pranks. "Don't worry—it's minor stuff."

"Does the sheriff know who's doing it?"

She shook her head. "New subject. What do you want for Christmas?"

He smiled. "Do you have any money to buy gifts?"

"Something small." She winked. "Maybe underwear or socks."

"That's okay. I don't need anything."

Usually her brother's I-want list was a page long. "What about a gas card for your car?"

"Yeah, that would be good." He squirmed on the seat.

"Are you nervous about your ride this afternoon?"

"Nah."

Right.

"Ladies and gentlemen, can I have your attention, please."

Luke and Hannah glanced at the loudspeaker hanging above their heads.

"All junior rodeo contestants report to the event sign-in table to pick up your numbers."

"I better go." Luke stood.

"Alonso and I will see you after the rodeo, okay?"

"Sure."

He turned away but stopped when she called after him. "Don't get hurt."

"That's the plan."

Hannah finished her water, then chucked the plastic bottle into a recycle bin and went to look for Alonso in the stands. He found her first.

"How was your visit with Luke?"

"He doesn't want to go back to his high school. He'd rather stay at the boys' ranch."

"I didn't want to leave, either. He'll be okay once he's home and gets into a routine." Alonso placed his hand against her lower back and followed her into the bleachers. When they were seated, he asked, "Are you hungry?"

"No, thanks. I ate a soft pretzel while I chatted with Luke."

"What's wrong?" He pressed the tip of his finger against the bridge of her nose. "You're frowning."

"I told Luke that I'd consider buying his half of the ranch once he graduates from high school." She sighed. "He doesn't want to be a rancher." She motioned to the arena. "He wants to rodeo." Maybe she shouldn't have said anything to Alonso. Now he'd worry about her and the baby being by themselves once Luke graduated.

She'd hardly slept the previous night because she fretted over the possibility of Alonso proposing to her—out of guilt. Hannah had seen firsthand the damage an unplanned pregnancy could do to a family. Her father had got Luke's mother pregnant by accident, and then Hannah's mother had filed for divorce.

If she and Alonso married just because of the baby, their relationship would never last. She'd rather raise their child alone with one happy parent than two unhappy parents.

"Ladies and gentlemen, welcome to the eighth annual junior rodeo competition at the Alamosa Fairgrounds!" The fans stomped their boots and whistled. "You'll see we have a few new names in the lineup this afternoon. Let's give a warm Los Alamos welcome to the five buckaroos from the Juan Alvarez Ranch for Boys."

The crowd applauded, and then a teenage girl rode into the arena carrying the American flag. She stopped her horse in front of the grandstand. The National Anthem played over the loudspeakers and the crowd sang along.

"Up first today in the saddle-bronc competition is Michael Foster. Cowboy Michael will do his best to tame Lickety-split, a bronc from the Del Mar Ranch in Las Cruces."

The gate opened and Lickety-split sprang into the arena. Hannah had been to a few rodeos through the years and the horses being used today were smaller and less athletic than the ones ridden by seasoned rodeo veterans. Fine by her. She didn't want Luke getting hurt.

Michael kept his seat until the buzzer, then launched himself into the air and landed on his face in the dirt. He was slow to get up, stopping once on the way back to the chute to spit the dirt out of his mouth.

"Not a bad showing for his first rodeo! Let's see what the judges think."

"The score will flash over there." Alonso leaned close and pointed across the arena. The scent of cologne and warm man surrounded her, and she inhaled, resisting the urge to bury her face in his neck. There were moments like now when the gnawing hunger to kiss him almost overwhelmed her. No matter what path their relationship took, she'd always be attracted to him.

"The judges liked Michael Foster's ride. He earned an eighty-two! Congratulations, cowboy!"

After the applause died down, the announcer introduced Hannah's brother. "Up next is Luke Buck, another contender from the Juan Alvarez Ranch for Boys. This is also Luke's first official go-round."

Hannah crossed her fingers when Luke climbed on top of his bronc.

"Luke will try to tame Midnight Express this afternoon. This is the bronc's first rodeo, too."

The gate opened and Midnight Express jumped out, bucked once, then froze.

"Folks, it looks as if our bronc might be shy today. Let's make a little noise and see if we can rile him." The fans jumped up and down on the aluminum bleachers, creating a deafening din. All of a sudden Midnight Express reared and Luke slid off, landing on his butt in the dirt.

"Well, now, that wasn't fair, was it?" the announcer said. The fans booed the horse.

"Looks as though the judges are going to give Luke and Midnight Express another chance." The rodeo helpers walked the horse back to the chute and Luke climbed the rails and slid onto the horse's back. This time when the gate opened, the bronc bucked.

Hannah held her breath as Luke flopped from side to side. He hung on until the buzzer, then jumped for safety. His landing wasn't much better than Michael's. She mumbled a silent prayer of thanks when Luke waved his hat to the crowd and walked back to the cowboy ready area.

"Not bad," Alonso said.

"Luke Buck earned an eighty-one for his efforts and sits in second place!"

"I have no idea why men believe getting whiplash is exciting," Hannah said.

"Let's congratulate him." Alonso took her hand and they left the stands before the other boys finished riding.

When they arrived behind the chutes, Luke and Michael were high-fiving each other and laughing.

Luke noticed her and Alonso and raced over to them. "Did you see me?"

"We did!" She hugged Luke. "Congratulations on making the buzzer."

"It wasn't a great ride, but it was fun."

"Let's hope you get a better draw next time," Alonso said.

Luke exchanged a private look with Michael, then lowered his voice. "Can Michael come to the ranch for Christmas? All the boys are leaving for the week but Michael has nowhere to go."

"What do you mean he has nowhere to go?" she asked.

"His dad's in prison and no one knows where his mom is."

Hannah felt bad for the teen. And relieved. If Michael kept Luke occupied during the winter break, her brother wouldn't be tempted to get into trouble. "Sure, Michael can stay with us."

"You don't have to buy us any presents. We don't care about that stuff."

Hannah suspected Luke had already invited Michael to join them for the holiday. Luke brought his friend over and introduced him, then Hannah said, "We'd love for you to spend Christmas with us, Michael. I'm sure Alonso will appreciate the extra help with chores."

Luke groaned, and Alonso grasped both boys' shoulders. "I'll keep you busy day and night."

"Maria said you can pick us up next Thursday."

"Okay," she said.

"Thanks, Hannah." Luke and Michael went back to the chute to cheer their friends on.

"I have my doctor's appointment that Thursday," Hannah said.

"I'll get the boys." He nodded to the arena. "You want to stick around for the rest of the rodeo or head back?"

Hannah's gaze swung to Luke and Michael goofing off with the other teens. She wanted Luke to have fun and not worry that he had to spend more time with her. "We can leave."

When they reached the pickup, Alonso said, "How about we look for a Christmas tree today?"

Hannah hadn't planned on spending money on a tree, but now that Luke was bringing a friend home she should at least try to fake a little holiday cheer. "Okay." Hannah squirmed into a comfortable position on the seat. All she'd done today was sit on her keister, but keeping her eyes open any longer was impossible.

Chapter Eleven

Alonso glanced between Hannah and the road. She'd fallen asleep minutes after leaving the rodeo in Los Alamos. He attributed her sleepiness not only to her pregnancy but to worry. He wanted to reassure her that everything was going to be okay, but it wasn't.

The Blue Bison was struggling financially. Hannah was about to become a single mother. In two years there was a good chance Luke would hit the rodeo circuit and leave all the responsibility for the ranch on Hannah's shoulders. And then there was him—the father of her baby was scared senseless.

No matter which way he twisted his thinking, there was no getting over the fact that they were bringing a baby into a world full of hatred and tragedy. He'd seen too much bad to believe their child could escape every evil. What if something happened to the baby that was beyond their control—an illness or accident?

Granted, he'd seen more bad than good because of his chosen career and time spent in the military. But there was bad everywhere—even Hannah couldn't escape it two hours outside of Albuquerque. Her ranch had been the target of vandals. And no matter where you lived, whether it was a major metropolitan area or a small town like Paradise, people were people and not all of them were good. Their child might be able to avoid inner-city gangs and violence in school but there were rural thugs who preyed on people, too.

As a trauma surgeon he could save victims of violence and tragic accidents, but he couldn't prevent them. There was no running away from life, no matter how far he walked. He had a lot of thinking to do when he returned to the hospital after the holidays. Maybe a break from Hannah would help him see things in a different light.

When he drove into Paradise, he parked next to the Christmas-tree lot adjacent to the gas station. "Wake up, sleepyhead."

Hannah's lashes fluttered open and their gazes clashed. In that unguarded moment she smiled, and his heart melted when he got a taste of what it would be like to see her smile every day. "Sorry." She yawned. "I was more tired than I thought."

"Ready to find a tree?"

She unbuckled her belt and peered through the windshield. "None of them looks very good."

He chuckled. "We can't be picky. We're late getting into the Christmas game." He walked around the pickup and opened her door.

An older man with a grizzled face greeted them. "Howdy, folks. I'll take ten bucks off the price if you buy one today."

Alonso studied the evergreens and said, "They look like something Charlie Brown would drag home." Hannah's belly laugh lightened the mood. It was amazing how her smiling eyes could improve his outlook. "What about that one?" He walked over to a tree with a gaping hole on one side. "You can face this side toward the living room corner. No one would know half the tree is missing."

"What about the gun closet?"

"I'll move it."

"Seems like a lot of work for half a tree."

"It will look better once it's decorated. And if you have outdoor lights, I'll string them across the porch."

"How much is the tree?"

"I'm buying it," he said.

"You don't have—"

"It's only fair that I pay, because you'll be stuck taking down the decorations."

"Fine. You buy the tree." This time when Hannah smiled her eyes didn't sparkle. "I'll wait in the truck."

Alonso paid for the sickly evergreen, then used the twine the salesman provided to secure it in the truck bed. As soon as they arrived at the ranch, he set the tree on the porch.

"I need to check the herd before it gets dark," Hannah said.

"Want me to tag along?"

"No, I'll be fine. There's a tree stand in the attic."

Alonso watched Hannah drive off, wishing he hadn't mentioned her being stuck taking down the tree. His leaving was going to put a damper on Christmas.

What did you expect? She knows she can't count on you for the long haul.

Maybe so, but he had to find a way to make the holiday special because he wanted to see a smile on Hannah's face when he left her.

And he would leave.

Maybe if he told himself that over and over he'd finally believe it.

HANNAH BREATHED A sigh of relief when Alonso's image grew smaller in the rearview mirror. After he'd unloaded the tree, she'd got behind the wheel and driven off to check on the bison.

Alonso reminded her at every opportunity that he was leaving, but he couldn't hide the truth from her. It was there in his eyes each time he looked at her. He felt obligated to stay—for the baby's sake. When push came to shove, the man was not going to abandon her. As much as she appreciated his sense of duty toward her and the baby, she didn't want to hold him back from being what he needed to be—a trauma surgeon.

She was doing exactly what she wanted to do with her life and it wouldn't be fair if Alonso had to sacrifice his calling because they'd messed up and she'd ended up pregnant. Besides, they'd only been together a month and a half—they hardly knew each other.

You know the important things about Alonso—that's enough to build a relationship on. Maybe so, but staying together because of the baby would only carry the relationship so far—then what? Things would grow awkward between them and Hannah would eventually have to insist that he leave.

Hannah checked all the pastures, relieved when she found no signs of property damage. When she returned to the house she saw Alonso standing on a ladder stringing lights across the overhang. As she drove past the tractor behind the barn she noticed it sat at an odd angle. She parked by the porch, then admired Alonso's handiwork.

"That looks nice," she said.

"I found the lights in the attic when I was looking for the tree stand."

"Is the tree in the living room?"

"Yep, and so are the bins with the ornaments."

"Thanks."

"Hannah?"

"What?"

"There's a baby crib in the attic."

"That's Luke's."

"I can put it together if you want."

"Luke can help me with that later."

A long pause followed, then he said, "Sure."

"Alonso, does the tractor look as though it's sitting at an angle?" Maybe pregnancy hormones were affecting her vision, but she swore the machine leaned toward one side.

He climbed down the ladder and stared across the driveway. "Maybe. Let's go take a look."

When they reached the tractor they both gaped in disbelief. Two of the tires on one side were flat.

Alonso dropped to his knees and examined a wheel. "Looks as if someone shot out the tire."

A new tire cost upward of a thousand dollars. And now with a two-thousand-dollar insurance deductible she was screwed. She didn't have that kind of money lying around. She removed her cell phone from her jeans pocket and contacted the sheriff. He was out on a call so she left a message with Sandy.

"I'm sorry, Hannah."

There was that look in his eyes again—the one that said he couldn't leave her to face her troubles by herself. As much as she wanted to cry right now at this latest turn of events, she had to remain strong. "I wish I knew why I'm being targeted. Good grief, I don't have any enemies."

"You sure Seth Markham and his father aren't behind this? They want your ranch. Maybe they think you'll get fed up and sell out if they keep nickel-and-diming you."

"They'd never do anything illegal and risk losing their own property." As they walked back to the house, Hannah asked, "How would you like homemade hot chocolate while we decorate the tree?"

"I've never had homemade hot chocolate."

"Then, it's about time you tasted the real stuff." They went into the house and he showed her the tree. "You're right. The corner is the perfect spot for it." Too bad she couldn't stand in a corner and make the hole in her heart disappear.

ALONSO UNHITCHED THE flatbed trailer next to the barn, then parked the pickup by the house. It had been in the low forties when he'd left to feed the herd at dawn. Now the sun was out, but a brisk wind kept the temperature from climbing and made the ache in his back worse. Now that Luke was home from the boys' ranch, he and Michael had set up camp in Luke's bedroom and Alonso slept on the couch. Hannah had offered to clear out some of the junk in the third bedroom and bring in the cot from the barn but he didn't want her to go to all that trouble for a few nights.

When he entered the kitchen, the aroma of fresh-baked cookies filled the air. For an instant he caught a glimpse of what future Christmases would be like for his child— with a single mother struggling to make the day special. Hannah would perform all the holiday duties—baking cookies, decorating the house and helping with school parties and plays. But she'd do it alone.

Didn't he want better for his child than what he'd

experienced growing up with a single mother? "I don't think it'll warm up much today," he said, alerting Hannah to his presence.

"The weatherman on the radio said there's a chance of snow flurries tonight." She smiled—that same forced smile she'd given him the day they'd returned from the boys' ranch at Thanksgiving. If he didn't know better, he'd almost believe Hannah was too cheery, especially for a woman in her situation. Then again, maybe she was putting on a front for Luke and Michael because it was Christmas.

"I bet the boys would like it to snow." He glanced down the hallway. "Are they up yet?"

"They're out in the barn, feeding Buster and cleaning his stall."

Alonso was relieved that the teens were following through with their promise to help out with chores. "I bought these for the guys yesterday when I went into town." He removed the iTunes gift cards from his pocket. "Do you have a box for them or wrapping paper?"

"You didn't have to get the boys a gift," she said.

"I wanted to." He suspected Christmas gifts weren't in Hannah's budget this year.

"I know they'll appreciate them." She went back to rolling out the cookie dough on a cutting board.

Today was Sunday—Christmas Eve. Hannah had gone to her medical appointment in Albuquerque three days ago and insisted everything was fine.

"You didn't say much about your doctor visit on Thursday."

"I told you. He said I'm healthy. And the baby's healthy, too."

He gave her a minute to elaborate. When she didn't, he asked, "Did your blood work turn out okay?"

"All good. He wants me to come in for an ultrasound in February."

"I'll go with you if you want."

She stopped rolling the dough. "You'll be working at the hospital by then."

He tried to read between the lines but couldn't figure out if Hannah wanted him to go with her or if she was trying to give him an out. He didn't have time to ask, because the back door opened and the boys joined them in the kitchen.

"It's Christmas Eve," Luke announced.

Hannah laughed. "That's right. Santa Claus is coming tonight."

"Can Michael and I go into town and rent some movies?"

"Sure. Pick out a Christmas movie we can watch later," Hannah said.

Alonso caught the secret look the teens exchanged and worried they had more on their mind than renting movies. "I'll drive you guys into Paradise."

"That's okay. I'm gonna take the Civic," Luke said.

"Don't stay out too long. I'm making a big pot of chili and corn bread for lunch."

"Ms. Hannah, can I have a cookie before we leave?" Michael asked.

She waved the teen over to the counter. "Frosted or unfrosted?"

"Frosted." He picked a snowman then bit its head off. "These are awesome, thanks."

"Take a few for the road," she said.

The boys loaded up on cookies and after they left,

Alonso said, "I have an errand to run. Do you mind if I use the pickup?" Alonso wanted to make sure the boys really intended to drive into town. The last thing Hannah needed to deal with was Luke running into an old friend and getting into trouble with him.

"Sure. Take your time."

Alonso gave the Civic a head start before he took off in the pickup. When he arrived in Paradise, he spotted the car at the convenience store. Relieved Luke had kept his word about renting movies, Alonso parked farther down the street in front of the drugstore—far enough away that Luke wouldn't notice the truck when he and Michael got ready to leave town.

Alonso hadn't bought Hannah a present when he'd picked out the gift cards for the boys because he didn't know what to buy her. He stared at the flashing neon sign advertising an ATM inside. She could use extra cash but she'd never accept money from him—not even if he claimed it was for his room and board. He'd lived with her since the beginning of November yet he didn't even know her favorite color.

But you know her dream.

And her dream of keeping the Blue Bison afloat was becoming more iffy with each passing day. As long as he remained on the job as a trauma surgeon he was confident he could help Hannah keep the ranch. He had a nice nest egg saved from his time in the military— she could use the money to pay a hired hand to help her with the herd. And he'd send her generous child-support checks each month. He wasn't worried about her financial situation. And until now it hadn't occurred to him that one day Hannah might meet another man who'd be more than willing to take care of her and his baby. What if she fell in love with the hired help? Did he want another man raising his child?

You don't have the right to be possessive of Hannah or the baby if you turn your back on them.

He wanted to be there for them both, but old fears crept in, undermining his confidence.

He glanced down the street and noticed a sign advertising Puppies 4-Sale with an arrow pointing at the feed store. Alonso went to take a look. The bell on the door announced his arrival. "Hey, Mel. You look a lot better than the last time I saw you."

The store manager grinned. "Shoulder's a little sore if I do too much, but thanks to you, I can move it just fine." He demonstrated by raising his arm in the air. "Gave the missus quite a scare, though."

"I imagine you did." Alonso glanced down the aisles.

"Whatcha looking for?" Mel asked.

"I saw that sign for puppies down the block."

"Burt's dog had another litter. There's one left." Mel pointed behind him. "He's sitting in the storage room, watching the TV."

Alonso poked his head inside the room. An old man sat in a lawn chair puffing on a cigarette. "Howdy."

"I saw your sign across the street."

"I was hoping to find this pup a home before Christmas. You interested?"

"What kind of dog?"

"Bullmastiff. It's a male."

No wonder the man was having trouble finding the puppy a home. "He'll be a big dog once he's full grown." Maybe too big for Hannah to handle.

"His sire is two and a half feet tall at the shoulder and weighs 170 pounds."

"I don't know much about the breed other than its size."

"You won't find a dog more loyal to family than a bullmastiff. They're fearless protectors."

Alonso liked the sound of that. "Are they easy to train?"

"If you work with them. Once you develop a bond, they won't leave your side."

"Any drawbacks?"

The old man chuckled. "They drool a lot."

"What about babies? Are they careful around little people?"

"Kids can tug their ears and crawl on their backs. The dog'll tolerate a lot, but they don't like strangers. Watch 'em when new people come by."

"How are they with horses and other ranch animals?"

"They'll protect them, too."

"Let me take a look at the puppy."

The old man opened the dog crate and removed the puppy. Alonso held the pup and the dog wagged its tail, then licked his face.

"He likes you," Burt said.

The dog had a cream-colored coat, black ears and a black snout. "I'm guessing they eat a lot."

"Yep."

He'd have to make sure his child-support checks covered dog food and vet bills. "How many pups were in the litter?"

"Just three. The other two were females."

"What kind of shots does he need?"

"I had the puppies checked out by a vet a week ago. They've had their first round of vaccinations already and they were dewormed." He reached into his pocket and held out a business card. "Vet's local."

"How much?"

"I got a thousand a piece for the females but I'll take nine hundred for the male."

Nine hundred?

"He's a purebred. His papers are right here." He patted his coat pocket. "You ask any breeder who shows these dogs and they'll tell you I gave you a deal."

"I don't plan to show the dog."

"Guess I could take eight hundred, then."

Alonso stared into the puppy's eyes. *Are you worth eight hundred dollars?* The dog licked Alonso's nose and that sealed the deal. He handed the puppy to the old man. "I'll be back with the money in a minute."

Alonso crossed the street and ducked inside the drugstore. After withdrawing money from the ATM, he asked the clerk for a large empty box. While she searched for him, he perused the Christmas aisle and picked out a red bow. Then he paid for his purchase and left.

"You can take this blanket with you." Burt stuffed the cloth into the cardboard box, then held out a plastic grocery bag. "Puppy food and teething toys."

"Thanks." Alonso took the box with the puppy and set it on the checkout counter. "Looks as if I'll need more puppy food."

"Pet supplies are in the back corner," Mel said.

Two hundred dollars later, Alonso had purchased three large bags of puppy food, a water bowl, food bowl and more chew toys, along with a horse blanket and a sturdy kennel in case Hannah wanted to crate the puppy in the house when she wasn't there.

As soon as he'd loaded the supplies in the truck and set the box with the puppy on the front seat, the boys walked out of the convenience store with sodas and a handful of movies. He felt bad for doubting the boys and waited a few minutes until after they'd left before heading out of town.

When he arrived at the ranch, he parked behind the barn and sneaked the dog inside. He set up the crate in the storage room and gave the puppy food and water before heading inside to eat lunch with Hannah and the boys. After the meal, he excused himself to check on the dog. He went back and forth between the house and the barn all day and evening, checking on the pup. Later when everyone went to bed, he'd bring the dog inside. He wanted Hannah to find the puppy under the tree Christmas morning.

Chapter Twelve

"Shh…"

Alonso held his breath and kept his eyes closed.

"Be quiet." Luke's voice carried into the living room, where Alonso pretended to sleep.

Two pairs of sock feet crept along the hallway. The back door opened then closed. Alonso sat up and shoved his feet into his boots, then checked on the puppy—fast asleep in the crate hidden behind the couch. By the time he stepped outside, the taillights on the Civic were fading fast.

He grabbed Hannah's keys from the hook by the door, shrugged into his coat, then took off after them. Damn Luke for sneaking out during the wee hours of Christmas morning. With luck he'd catch the teens before they got into trouble.

When Alonso reached the main road there was no sign of the car. His first thought was to drive into town, but his gut insisted the teens were headed west, so he turned right and hit the gas. He'd gone a mile when he noticed a vehicle parked on the shoulder of the road up ahead.

He slowed as he approached, saw it was a pickup,

then sped by. But as he passed he caught sight of the Civic parked on the shoulder with its lights off.

Damn it, Luke. The kid better not be buying drugs. He shifted into Reverse and hit the gas. Someone hopped into the truck and sped off, leaving Luke standing alone on the road. Alonso parked in front of the Civic. Michael sat in the front seat of the car and stayed there when he spotted Alonso. Smart kid.

"It's not what you think," Luke said.

"So you weren't buying drugs?"

"No!"

"Then, what the hell are you doing out here at two in the morning?"

"I can't tell you."

"If you can't tell me then that means you were up to no good."

"It's not like that. I'm trying to fix something."

Alonso stared long and hard at the teen, who appeared shaken. "Who was that guy you were talking with?"

"I can't tell you."

"Fine, but you're going to tell your sister. I'll follow you home."

Shoulders slumped, Luke returned to the car, made a U-turn and drove back to the ranch, Alonso riding his bumper.

When they pulled into the yard it was two thirty. "I'll give you until after opening presents in the morning to talk to Hannah. If you don't, then I'll say something."

The boys went into the house and retreated to Luke's bedroom. Alonso locked up, checked the puppy—still fast asleep—then stretched out on the couch and stared into the dark. Hannah was pregnant with his child. Her brother was still up to no good. And the sheriff had yet to catch the culprits responsible for destroying her property.

There was no way he could leave Hannah in such a mess.

HANNAH WOKE TO a quiet house Christmas morning. After taking a quick shower she threw on a pair of jeans, which she discovered pinched her around the waist. She tossed them aside and slipped into her comfy gray sweatpants and a pink sweatshirt. Shoving her feet into her rabbit-ear slippers she went downstairs and put a breakfast casserole and a pan of cinnamon rolls into the oven.

"Need help?"

She glanced over her shoulder, then swallowed a sigh. Alonso's sexy sleepy-eyed stare made her want to forget about food and go back to bed— with him. "No, thanks. Breakfast will be ready as soon as the boys are up."

He sat at the table.

"Orange juice?" she asked.

"Thanks."

She set the glass in front of him, then joined him. "I've decided to wait to tell Luke about the baby until after Michael and you leave."

He swirled the juice in the glass. "Don't you think I should be here when you break the news?"

"No, I'd like to handle this my way." *Because Luke will want you to stay.* She didn't give him a chance to argue with her. "I thought you parked the truck by the barn last night."

"I took a drive earlier this morning."

She quirked an eyebrow, but didn't pry. "Remind me to tell Luke that we need to meet with Principal Connelly over break and get his class schedule for next semester."

The timer on the oven dinged and she removed the rolls, placed one on a plate and handed it to Alonso. "I'll be right back." She was halfway down the hall when the boys stepped from Luke's room.

"What smells so good, Ms. Hannah?" Michael asked.

"Cinnamon rolls. Get 'em while they're warm."

The boys joined Alonso at the table and ate in silence. Ten minutes later the rolls were gone.

"Let's open gifts while the casserole is baking," she said. They all headed to the living room. "Michael, you're our guest. You go first." Hannah handed him an envelope.

Michael gaped. "I didn't expect a gift."

"It's not much," she said, wishing there had been more money in the budget for gifts, but the insurance deductibles had wiped out her savings.

"Wow, thanks a lot!" Michael studied the gift card. "I'm gonna buy a new riding glove with this."

"Here's yours, Luke." Hannah had given the same thing to her brother.

"Thanks," Luke said.

"I got you guys something, too." Alonso reached beneath the couch cushion and handed each teen a smaller envelope.

"iTunes gift cards!" Luke said.

"Cool," Michael said. "Thanks, Mr. Marquez."

"Yeah, thanks, Alonso."

"What did you get—" Luke sniffed the air and made an ugly face. "Did someone fart?"

"Luke!" Hannah rolled her eyes.

"Can't you smell that?" Luke asked.

"I think I know what it is." The three stared at Alonso. "Hannah's Christmas gift." He ducked behind the couch.

"What's back there?" Hannah asked.

"This little guy." He stood with the puppy in his hand. Hannah gasped.

"You bought my sister a puppy!" Luke shouted.

"I hope no one is allergic to dogs," Alonso said.

"Is it a he or a she?" Luke asked.

"It's a male bullmastiff." He handed the puppy to Hannah and she cuddled it against her.

"How big will he get?" she asked.

"Close to a 150 pounds."

"That's huge," Michael said.

"They're gentle giants and used as guard dogs. He'll protect his family and his breeder said he'll be good with ba—kids of all ages."

Hannah breathed a sigh of relief when Alonso caught himself before he said *babies*.

"I bought a stockpile of food and the puppy has already had his first round of shots."

Although it was thoughtful of Alonso to want her to have a dog for protection and she appreciated that he'd stocked up on supplies for her, how could she afford to keep the animal once he left? And it wasn't only the financial cost of owning and caring for a pet that worried her—the dog would always be a reminder of Alonso.

"Let me hold him." Luke took the puppy from her. "Can we play with him outside?"

"Sure." Once the boys left the house, Hannah said, "As much as I appreciate the thought, I can't afford a dog." Taking care of the bison cost her plenty already.

"I'll pay for its food and vet bills."

She trusted Alonso to keep his word, but what if his work situation changed and he couldn't follow through on his promise?

"You need a dog, Hannah. It'll be just you and the baby once Luke takes off after he graduates from high school."

A knot formed in her throat when she imagined herself alone with a dog and a child. That was not the future she'd envisioned, but maybe Alonso was right. She would feel safer if she had a dog for protection. "Thank you."

Alonso hugged her and she buried her face in the crook of his neck. Why did he have to be the man she wanted but couldn't have?

"Hannah?"

"Hmm…"

"Luke has something to tell you."

"What?"

He stared into her eyes. "The reason I moved the pickup was because the boys left the house at two in the morning and I followed them."

Her heart dropped into her stomach. "Where did they go?"

"I caught up with them a couple of miles down the road. Luke was talking to a guy on the shoulder, but he took off when I stopped. Luke wouldn't say what he was doing out there but I made him promise to talk to you about it."

And earlier Hannah had woken up believing this Christmas would be a new start for her and Luke, but nothing had changed. Her brother was back to his wild ways. "I better find out what he's up to."

"Send Michael inside with the puppy," Alonso said. "He can help me clean the dog crate while you and Luke chat."

"Thanks." Hannah trudged outside as if the weight of her bison herd rested on her shoulders.

"MICHAEL," HANNAH SAID when she stepped onto the porch, where the boys were playing with the dog. "Would you take the puppy inside and help Alonso clean the crate?"

"Sure." Michael sent Luke a panicked look before disappearing with the dog.

Luke shuffled his feet but wouldn't make eye contact with her. "I hear you and Michael sneaked out of the house earlier this morning," she said.

Her brother's hand shook when he pushed the hair off his forehead. Was it that bad? "You told Alonso you weren't buying drugs. Was that the truth?"

Luke nodded, but remained closemouthed.

"Who was the guy Alonso saw you with?"

Tears welled in her brother's eyes and Hannah's chest grew tight. She hadn't seen her brother cry in forever—he hadn't even shed a tear at his mother's or their father's funeral.

"I did it because I thought you'd make me stay here and help out on the ranch after I graduated."

"But I told you I wouldn't."

"I know that now, but—"

"Hold on." The ranch was her dream—whether she kept it or not had nothing to do with Luke. "I won't lie. It will be tough not having your help, but if rodeo is your future, I won't stand in your way."

"But you kind of are."

"How am I keeping you from following your dream?"

"You won't leave this stupid ranch, so I'm gonna have to stay."

She raised her arms in the air. "Why do you believe you have to stay? I already told you that I'd try to buy out your share if and when you knew for sure you were going to rodeo."

"I can't leave you alone. Something might happen to you."

That Luke worried about her warmed Hannah's heart. "Nothing is going to happen to me. I've been taking care of myself and you for a long time. I'll be fine when you leave."

"But you'll be all alone."

Not for long.

"And you'll be lonely."

Hannah couldn't stand the anguished look on her brother's face. "I don't mind being alone."

"But you've always been there for me. It's my turn to be there for you."

Tears filled Hannah's eyes. To hear Luke acknowledge the sacrifices she'd made for him made her love him all the more.

"If I rodeo, I can't be there for you. That's why I did it."

"Did what?"

"I paid a guy to vandalize the ranch."

Hannah sucked in a quick breath.

"The guys who tried to rob the convenience store hooked me up with this person who does stuff for money."

No. No, Luke. No!

"Where did you get the money to pay him?" Her brother didn't even have a job.

"I've been saving my allowance and I borrowed money from Connor."

Connor worked at a pizza parlor after school and on weekends. "How much did you take from him?"

"A thousand dollars."

Hannah felt faint and sat down in the rocker.

"I had to pay the guy three hundred dollars each time he did something."

Did something? That was how her brother referred to the vandalism? "Luke, those weren't just pranks. The damage cost me—us—thousands of dollars, not to mention our insurance premium went up as well as the deductible."

Luke paced back and forth. "I thought you'd want to give the ranch up after all that stuff happened." He sniffed. "Then I wouldn't feel guilty when I went on the rodeo circuit."

Her brother really hadn't thought this through. "Where did you think I'd go if I no longer had the ranch?"

He stared at her with wide eyes. "With me. We'd travel the circuit together."

Any anger she felt toward her brother evaporated when she looked into his pleading eyes. It had been just the two of them for so long—even when their father had still been alive, Luke had come to her for everything. "You might feel that way now, but I guarantee by the time you turn eighteen you'll be ready to strike out on your own and you will not want your big sister tagging along." He didn't even protest when she squeezed his hand.

"So you met with that guy last night to tell him to hit us up again?"

"I told him to stop. That I didn't need his help anymore."

"Why?"

"Because I realized something when I was at the boys' ranch."

"What's that?"

"That you've sacrificed a lot for me."

She opened her mouth to protest, but he cut her off. "I know you wanted to go to college, but then my mom died and you didn't want to leave me all alone with Dad." He sucked in a deep breath. "So I'm not gonna leave you all alone, either. If you don't want to sell the ranch, then I'll stay here after graduation."

She wanted to box his ears for what he'd done, but she couldn't love her brother more than she did right now. "Luke, I love you, and I love you even more for wanting to stay here and protect me, but I'm a grown woman. We each have to live our own lives."

"Are you just saying that or do you really mean it?" he asked.

"I really mean it."

"Then, you won't be mad if I tell you I want to go to a rodeo camp next summer?"

She smiled. "I won't be mad, but we might have a problem paying for the camp."

"I'm sorry, Hannah. I'll get a job and pay back all the money you had to spend to fix stuff."

"That sounds like a fair deal." If she could, Hannah would save the money and give it back to Luke once he graduated, so he'd have cash for the road.

"Are you gonna tell the sheriff what I did?"

"No, you're going to talk to the sheriff."

"But—"

"You have to tell the truth, Luke, or else it will catch up with you someday."

"I don't know the guy's real name. He told me to call him Todd."

"Tell the sheriff what you know and we'll deal with the consequences together."

"Will I go to jail?"

"I hope not." It wouldn't hurt for Luke to worry a little. What he'd done was a serious offense.

"When are we gonna see the sheriff?"

"Tomorrow."

Luke stared at the ground, wiping at his eyes.

"I wish you'd have talked to me and shared your concerns before you went to this extreme."

"I'm sorry." He hugged Hannah.

"Let's go inside. It's freezing out here."

Hannah excused herself to take a nap. Ignoring Alonso's questioning look, she retreated to her bedroom, where she sat on the bed and cried. Cried for herself. For Luke. For the baby. And for Alonso. Her little family was a mess. It didn't matter that Luke would leave one day and Alonso would leave soon. They were still a family.

"HANNAH?" ALONSO STOOD outside her bedroom door, a plate of crackers and cheese in one hand, a water bottle in the other.

"I'm sleeping."

Obviously she wasn't if she'd answered him. It had been two hours since Luke and Hannah had talked and she'd retired to her bedroom. Luke and Michael had taken the puppy into Luke's room to watch movies.

"Mind if I come in?" He tested the knob, found it open and entered the room. Hannah sat on the edge of the bed with red-rimmed eyes and her blond hair mussed. She looked like a waif, hardly old enough to be pregnant. "I thought you might be hungry." He sat on the mattress next to her and she helped herself to a piece of cheese.

"Thanks."

He handed her the water bottle. "Did Luke tell you why he sneaked out?"

"Yes."

By the looks of her, whatever Luke had done hadn't been good. "If you don't want to tell me, you don't have to." The pain in her eyes was so raw it stole his breath.

"Luke was paying that guy you saw him with to trash the ranch."

"Why?"

She swiped at the fresh tears that ran down her cheeks. "He feels guilty about leaving me here alone if he joins the rodeo circuit after high school. He was hoping I'd get fed up with the pranks and put the ranch up for sale and tag along with him."

Alonso was dumbfounded. He'd never expected Luke to be involved in the vandalism. No wonder Hannah was a wreck.

"Luke met with that guy last night to tell him to stop."

"Why?"

"Because he realized what he was doing wasn't the right way to pay me back for all the years I've stood by him." She waved a hand in the air. "I'm all the family he has left and he was worried about leaving me alone."

The image of Luke, Hannah and the baby standing together as a family drifted in front of Alonso's eyes, and a strong yearning to be part of that circle gripped his gut.

"We're driving into Paradise tomorrow to talk to the sheriff." She leaned her head against his shoulder and he slid his arm around her. Now that there would be no more threats against the ranch, Alonso felt better about leaving Hannah at the end of the month. "Are you sure this ranch is what you want?"

"This is my home, Alonso. I can't see myself doing anything else."

Maybe if his mother had been around more often, he'd think of the barrio as his home, but it would always be the place he'd wanted to escape from.

"Will you drive Michael back to the boys' ranch before you leave?"

It was the least he could do for her. "Sure. And why don't you make up a list of last-minute things I can help with before I go."

"That would be great, thanks."

He walked to the door. "When you feel up to it, come downstairs. The boys want to know what you're going to name the dog."

"I still can't believe you bought me a Christmas puppy."

"I probably should have asked. If you want, I can find the dog another home."

"We'll keep the puppy. Hopefully Luke will become attached to him and have a reason to come home and visit more often once he starts rodeoing."

Alonso left the room, closing the door behind him. Luke met him at the bottom of the stairs. "Is she okay?"

"She'll be down in a little while."

"Did she tell you?"

"Yes."

The teen dropped his gaze. "I hurt her pretty bad."

"Yes, you did."

Luke looked miserable.

"You can make it up to your sister by doing your chores and helping out more around the ranch."

"I'm going to."

"She loves you, Luke."

"I know." He went back into the kitchen and Alonso heard the boys trying to teach the puppy to sit.

Luke had a lot to make up for, but then so did Alonso—the difference was that Luke would stay and earn Hannah's forgiveness. Alonso intended to run away and pray that one day Hannah might find it in her heart to forgive him for bailing on her and their child.

Chapter Thirteen

"Thank you for seeing us, Sheriff Miller." Hannah sat down and Luke took the chair next to her. "I appreciate you coming in the day after Christmas."

"Not a problem. I had a phone call to make." He smiled at Luke. "Are you ready to return to school next semester?"

"Yes, sir."

"After you phoned, Hannah, I asked Principal Connelly to meet with us, but he's out of town for a few more days."

"We're not here to discuss Luke returning to class after the winter break," Hannah said.

The sheriff's eyebrows rose. "Oh?"

"Luke has something he needs to tell you." Hannah nudged her brother in the arm. Luke was nervous, and to be honest, he should be. She might have let him off the hook for what he'd done, but that didn't mean the sheriff would go as easy on him.

"I'm listening, Luke."

"I know who vandalized our ranch."

The sheriff straightened in his chair. "Who?"

"Me."

The sheriff's eyes widened and his mouth sagged open.

"I mean, not me, but I'm the one who paid a guy to…" Luke dropped his gaze.

Hannah took pity on her brother. "Luke and I had a misunderstanding, Sheriff. And instead of talking to me, Luke took matters into his own hands, hoping he could convince me to sell the ranch. Luke realized his mistake and that he'd handled things badly and has since told this person to stop vandalizing the ranch."

Sheriff Miller rubbed his hands down his face and stared at Luke. "I'm not sure what to say."

"I know what I did was wrong," Luke said. "And I'm gonna pay my sister back for all the damages."

"Who did you hire to do this, Luke?"

"A guy named Todd, but that's not his real name."

"How did you know to get in touch with this… Todd?"

Luke cast a quick glance at Hannah. "The guys who robbed the convenience store gave me his name."

"Kenny Potter and T. J. Templeton were involved in this?" the sheriff asked.

Luke sent Hannah a panic-stricken look.

"Sheriff, the other boys had nothing to do with the vandalism. Luke is taking full responsibility."

"It's not that simple, Hannah, when an insurance company is involved."

"I realize that. I intend to call them and explain the situation. We'll be paying for the damages."

The sheriff stared long and hard at Luke. "I've spent hours working on this case. My time could have been better spent helping someone in real need."

"Yes, sir."

"I don't want to press charges. And I'll settle things with the insurance company," Hannah said.

The sheriff leveled a stern look at her brother. "I better not hear of you becoming involved in anything like this again."

"Never again, sir."

"And I expect you to stay out of trouble in school next semester."

Luke nodded.

"I mean it. No more skipping classes. Not even one," the sheriff said.

"I won't. I'm all caught up with my homework assignments for the first semester."

The sheriff looked at Hannah, and she said, "Maria Fitzgerald has been in contact with Luke's guidance counselor at the high school. Luke won't have to repeat the fall semester."

"That's great news," the sheriff said. "What else did you do at the ranch?"

"Learned how to ride broncs, and I competed in a junior rodeo earlier this month."

"Is that right?"

Luke's face lit up with excitement as he told Sheriff Miller about the riding lessons Cruz Rivera had given him at the boys' ranch. Luke's rebellion had cost them plenty, but in the end they were going to be okay and her brother's future looked brighter than ever. Hannah wished she could say the same thing about her own.

"I appreciate you coming in here, Luke, and telling the truth." His gaze swung to Hannah. "I'd be happy to speak with your insurance company if you need me to."

"Thank you." Hannah stood and Luke shook the sheriff's hand.

"I hope you know what a lucky young man you are to have such an understanding sister."

Luke smiled at Hannah. "I know."

After they left the sheriff's office, Hannah stopped at the convenience store and asked Luke to run in and buy a gallon of milk. Then Luke nodded off during the drive home. When she pulled up to the house, she shook his shoulder and woke him.

"I'm really sorry, Hannah." He reached across the seat and gave her a hug.

"From here on out, things are going to get better." She had to believe that. "What are you and Michael planning to do today?"

"I was gonna ask Alonso if he'd go target shooting with Michael and me."

"I bet he would." She'd prefer that Alonso tag along with the boys. Hannah was confident that Luke knew how to handle a gun safely, but she worried that Michael might get hurt if they goofed off and weren't careful. "There's Alonso." He walked out of the barn.

"Alonso!" Luke called out. "Will you take Michael and me target shooting this afternoon?"

"Sure. As long as it's okay with your sister."

"I'm gonna tell Michael." Luke raced into the house.

"How did it go?"

Hannah would miss staring into Alonso's warm brown eyes. "Good. The sheriff isn't pressing charges and Luke gave his word that he'd stay out of trouble."

"I believe him. He's a good kid, Hannah."

"I think he and I have turned a corner," she said.

Alonso dropped his gaze to the ground, then expelled a sharp breath and looked her in the eye. "I've finished all the repairs, unless you have any more to add to the list you gave me."

He was ready to leave. "No, you've done more than enough."

"Maria phoned while you and Luke were in town. She'd like Michael to return tomorrow so she can work with him on his math. He didn't pass his last exam and she wants him to retake it. I told Maria I'd bring him back in the morning. I thought Luke might want to come along."

"Sure." If Michael left, there was no reason for Alonso to stay.

Except that Hannah still wasn't ready to say goodbye.

"CAN WE STAY AWHILE?" Luke asked when Alonso parked the Civic at the boys' ranch late Wednesday morning. "We want to ask Cruz if he'll let us ride a bronc."

"Sure. I'll walk down to the corral with you."

The ranch appeared empty—most of the boys they'd seen at Thanksgiving wouldn't be returning after the first of the year. Riley and Maria would enjoy a short break before the next group of juveniles descended on the property.

Cruz walked out of the barn and waved. "How was your Christmas?" he asked the boys.

"Good," they answered in unison.

Then Luke spoke. "Can we ride a bronc before Alonso and I have to leave?"

"Go into the barn and ask Nelson to pick out a horse for you." After the teens took off, Cruz asked, "How's Luke doing?"

"A lot better."

"What about Hannah? Is there still trouble at her ranch?"

"Not anymore." Alonso wouldn't share the details—

Hannah might not want others to know that her brother had been behind the vandalism.

Cruz glanced over his shoulder when Nelson escorted a horse out of the barn, the teens walking alongside him. "How are you holding up?"

Alonso frowned. "What do you mean?"

"Sara told me about Hannah. Is the baby yours?"

"How did Sara know Hannah was pregnant?"

"She said Hannah got sick when she was here at Thanksgiving."

Alonso thought back on that day. It all made sense now—having to stop on the way to the ranch so Hannah could use the bathroom. Her picking at the food on her plate and passing up dessert. Then her buying licorice and whatever else that had been in the brown paper bag on the way back to Paradise. If he had to guess, Hannah had purchased a pregnancy test at the gas station convenience store. "The baby's mine."

Cruz slapped Alonso on the back. "When's the wedding?"

"There isn't going to be one. And I'd appreciate you not saying anything about the baby to anyone. Hannah hasn't told Luke yet."

"Sure."

"I'm heading back to Albuquerque tomorrow," Alonso said.

Cruz looked at him funny but didn't ask why Alonso was taking off. "You ever run into any of the old gang in the barrio?"

"No." He avoided driving through his stomping grounds. There was nothing left there but bad memories. "Have you been back to Albuquerque since…"

"It's okay to say *prison*. Everyone thinks I'll fly into a rage if they mention I was behind bars."

"I wish that hadn't happened to you, Cruz."

"Me, too. But no matter how many times I go over it in my head, I wouldn't change a thing. If I hadn't gone with Vic that night, he might have gotten himself killed."

"I saw Vic at that youth rodeo in Los Alamos earlier this month. Can't believe he's bustin' broncs."

"Maria's been following his career. Vic sends his trophies to her for safekeeping."

"For a guy who never liked rodeo I'm surprised he's riding."

"He's damn good. Just missed the cut for the National Finals Rodeo in Vegas this year."

"Has he stopped at the ranch since you started working here?" Alonso asked.

"No."

Alonso could understand how it might be awkward for the two men after all that had happened in the past, but he hoped someday they'd be able to hash things out and put it behind them. Cruz and Vic had been friends before Alonso had joined the group. "Maybe I read him wrong," he said, "but Vic seemed as if he was just going through the motions. He didn't act like a cowboy who lived and died rodeo."

"Well, for a guy who doesn't like the sport, he's sure stuck with it long enough."

"Maybe you'll get the chance to see him ride next year," Alonso said.

Cruz remained silent, his gaze focused on the boys. Alonso got the feeling Vic's rodeo career was a touchy subject for Cruz. "I should have been there that night."

Cruz's gaze swung to Alonso. "I don't even remember why you weren't with us."

"I was in the emergency room with my sister. My mom was working and Lea had a bad asthma attack."

"How are your sisters these days?"

"Lea's married with kids. Carla's divorced." Cruz grew quiet again and Alonso decided they'd talked enough about the past. "I was hoping to speak to Maria before I leave."

"She's in the main house."

"Is Riley here?"

"Out of town on business."

"When the boys finish, will you send Luke up to the house?"

"Sure."

Alonso offered his hand. "Take care, Cruz. It was good seeing you again."

"I hope things work out for you, Hannah and the baby."

Alonso wanted that, too, he just wasn't sure how to make it happen. He walked to the house, then rang the bell. No one answered, so he tried the knob and the door swung open. "Maria?"

"In the kitchen!"

He wandered down a hallway that led to the kitchen at the back of the house.

"Alonso!" Maria popped off the bar stool and gave him a hug. "I didn't expect you for another hour." Holding him at arm's length, she studied his face. "What's the matter?"

"Everything." The word slipped from his mouth before he could stop it.

"I made a fresh pot of coffee a few minutes ago. Sit

down." She grabbed a mug from the cupboard and filled it with brew. "Are you hungry?" She didn't wait for him to answer before she set a plate of sweets in front of him.

He helped himself to a sugar cookie. "These are good, thanks."

"José made them. We're fortunate to have him cooking for the boys. They don't mind doing the dishes afterward because they want to eat whatever José made for dessert."

Alonso was content to let Maria chatter. She had a way of making people feel good and he could use a shot of self-esteem right now.

"I was just telling a friend of mine from the old neighborhood what a remarkable surgeon you are."

"I don't think I ever thanked you properly for pushing me toward college and med school."

"You always had it in you, Alonso. I just believed in you until you started believing in yourself."

Believe in yourself. He thought back to those days when he feared he wouldn't pass all his classes in college then later in med school. Maria had always been there, never allowing him to give up. And she'd been right—once he'd acknowledged that he was good enough to succeed at whatever he put his mind to, he'd never looked back.

So what the hell had happened to his confidence? How had he allowed himself to nurture such a dismal, dank outlook on life? Not even when he was a boy growing up in poverty had he believed the world was a hopeless place.

"Hannah told you the news, didn't she?" Maria said. He nodded.

She squeezed his hand. "And you don't believe you're ready to be a father."

"Yes. No." He shook his head. "It's complicated." If things were different—if he was different, he'd be excited about becoming a dad, but the idea of bringing a tiny human into such a crappy world scared him to death. Who in their right mind wanted the lifelong responsibility of keeping another human being safe and healthy when so much of what happened in the world was out of a person's control?

"When are you and Hannah getting married?"

"We're not." He winced at the look of disappointment in Maria's eyes.

"You don't love Hannah?"

Until now, Alonso hadn't allowed himself the luxury of analyzing his feelings for Hannah. He liked her. He admired her and he was attracted to her. He couldn't let his thoughts and feelings go beyond that, because he feared Hannah had the power to make him take a leap of faith and give the world a second chance. And he knew that second chances never worked out. He'd saved his buddies in the Army that fateful day, but their second chance had only lasted hours before it had been stolen from them.

"I won't let myself fall in love with Hannah." At Maria's surprised look he added, "The world sucks. I've witnessed too many horrors to believe in happy-ever-afters."

"Where did this pessimistic attitude come from?" She'd badger him until he spilled his guts.

"I think it's been in me my whole life. I just didn't realize it until I was in the Army. Growing up in the barrio I saw things most kids never see in their entire lives. I thought when I enrolled in college and then med school, I'd escape the doom and gloom of my past, but I didn't."

"I don't understand."

"I experienced some pretty rough stuff in Afghanistan. That's why I left the military early. I thought being back in the States and working in an ER would renew my faith in humanity, but it didn't. Every day at the hospital I see bad things happen to good people—people who are doing what they're supposed to do in life. When good people get killed by drunk drivers or shot standing at bus stops, you start thinking it doesn't matter that you're doing the right thing...the bad always wins over the good in the end."

He shoved a hand through his hair. "I took a leave from the hospital because there was no point in doing my job anymore. I was saving teenagers who went right back out on the streets and got themselves shot up again a week later."

Tears welled in Maria's eyes. Hell, he hadn't meant to make her cry. He gave her a hug. "I'm sorry. I don't mean to be such a downer."

"There are other things a man with a college degree can do." She sniffed.

"I'm good at saving people—it's just too bad the world is better at taking them away."

"It's not like you to turn your back on someone who needs you, Alonso."

"I'm not deserting Hannah. I intend to give her financial support and I'll be there to help out if she needs me." He'd help Hannah as long as he maintained an emotional distance from her. He couldn't afford to lose his heart to her and their child. God help him then if anything horrible happened to them.

"Forget about child-support payments," Maria said. "You never knew your father. Don't you want better for your son or daughter?"

"It's not as if I'm never going to see them." Even as he said the words, he knew they were a lie. He'd only visit Hannah and the baby if she reached out to him, and Hannah was a stubborn, strong woman—she wouldn't need him very often.

"I bet you'll feel differently once you hold the baby in your arms." Maria's cell phone rang and she glanced at the number. "Let me take this call. I'll be right back." As soon as she left the room, Alonso made a dash for the door.

He felt as if he'd gone ten rounds with Maria and she'd barely said a few sentences to him. When he stepped outside, he waved at Luke to meet him at the pickup. The kid talked the entire drive back to the ranch, but Alonso was battling his conscience and barely heard a word.

"Hey, Rambo, I'm home!" Luke raced into the living room, where Hannah was taking down the tree decorations. He dropped to his hands and knees on the floor and the puppy raced toward him, his big paws sliding on the wood.

Rambo was supposed to have been Hannah's dog, but the puppy had latched on to Luke, and the two were becoming best friends.

"Was it tough for Michael to go back to the ranch?" she asked.

"No. He likes it there."

"Good." She sent up a silent prayer of thanks that Maria and Riley Fitzgerald had put her brother on the right path.

Luke lifted Rambo up to his face and nuzzled the dog's nose. "You wanna go for a ride in the truck?" Rambo's little tail wagged. "He's smart, Hannah. He knows what going for a ride means."

"Why don't you grab a snack before you check on the bison?"

"I will." He got to his feet. "C'mon, Rambo." Luke skidded to a stop when Alonso appeared with his army bag slung over his shoulder. "Are you leaving?"

Alonso nodded. "It's time for me to hit the road again."

"But winter break isn't over yet."

"I have to be back at the hospital by January second." He had three days to make it to Albuquerque.

"I thought you were leaving tomorrow," Hannah said. She hadn't prepared herself for their goodbye.

Alonso shrugged. "There's still a few hours of daylight."

Luke's gaze swiveled between Hannah and Alonso. "But I thought you guys…you know…liked each other."

"We do," Hannah said, forcing a smile. "But Alonso's real job is saving people, not feeding bison." Alonso's gaze met hers, and in the brief instant before he looked away she saw yearning—the same longing she'd buried deep inside her.

"It kind of sucks." Luke smiled sheepishly. "I got used to you being here."

Me, too. Each night when Hannah drifted off to sleep, she imagined her, Alonso and the baby becoming a real family. Then she'd wake in the morning and realize it would never happen.

Luke offered Alonso his hand. "Thank you for everything."

"I'm glad things worked out for you, Luke. Do well in school and don't give your sister any grief."

"I won't. Michael's gonna come visit over my spring break. Maria said she'd drive him up here."

"Good. I'm sure your sister will appreciate the extra help with chores."

"Wait until Michael sees Rambo. He'll be huge by then." Luke stepped past Alonso. "Come back and visit us."

Hannah waited until the back door closed before she spoke. "After all the repairs you did, we should be in good shape for a while."

"Albuquerque isn't that far. If you need help, call me and I'll drive down." His stare pierced her. "I mean it." He removed a business card from his pants pocket and handed it to her. "That's the chief of staff's number. If you can't get hold of me, he'll make sure I get a message from you."

Hannah set the card on the coffee table. "If you wait until tomorrow, I can drive you back to Albuquerque."

His mouth curved in a half grin. "I made it this far hitching rides—I might as well return the same way."

"Let me at least give you a lift to the highway." She swept past him, and walked into the kitchen. Luke had left the keys to the Civic on the counter and she grabbed them on her way out the door. She didn't look over her shoulder for fear she'd cry if she made eye contact with him.

Alonso stowed his duffel in the backseat and they drove in silence. When Hannah reached the highway, she shifted into Park. They both stared out the windshield, neither saying a word.

This is what you want.

Not *want*. This was what had to be. Maybe if she told herself that enough times she'd believe it.

Alonso reached for the door handle. "Call if you need me. For anything."

She wanted to shout that she needed him for everything. "Okay," she whispered, battling tears. Damn it. She could do this alone. She'd taken care of herself and Luke for years before her father and Ruth had passed away. There was no doubt in her mind that she could take care of this baby by herself—it was just that she didn't want to do it alone. She wanted Alonso by her side, raising their child together.

He got out of the car and removed his duffel, then stuck his head back through the open passenger window. Their eyes connected and Hannah's breath caught at the sheen of moisture making his brown eyes sparkle. *You love me, Alonso. I know you do.*

"Be well, Hannah." He walked off before she found the courage to beg him to stay.

She kept her foot on the brake as she watched him stroll down the road. Not until he became a speck on the horizon did she put the car into Reverse and return to the house.

Only then did she realize Alonso had never looked back.

KEEP WALKING. DON'T STOP.

The urge to check over his shoulder to see if Hannah was still sitting in the car was more powerful than the rage he'd felt when his buddies had died in Afghanistan.

This is what you wanted.

The hell it was. He wanted to be with Hannah. He just couldn't, that was all. A horn honked and he jumped sideways, thinking he'd wandered onto the road. A blue Ford pulled onto the shoulder ahead of him. Doc Snyder. The old man lowered his window when Alonso approached. "Where are you headed?"

"Making my way back to Albuquerque."

The doctor eyed him suspiciously. "Why didn't Hannah give you a ride?"

"I needed time to think."

"About what?"

He didn't care for people poking their nose into his business. "Do me a favor and check on Hannah every now and then."

"Might have a problem with that."

"Why?"

"I put off that hip replacement I was supposed to have after Thanksgiving. I'm scheduled for surgery in three days. I'll be out of commission at least a month."

"Who's filling in for you at the clinic?"

"A doctor friend from Gallup. But he can only visit the clinic one day a week." Doc narrowed his eyes. "You wouldn't by chance know a doctor who'd be willing to help out my friend?"

The temptation to stay near Hannah was powerful, but if he didn't return to the hospital he could kiss his job goodbye. An image of Hannah large with child—his child—flashed before his eyes. He couldn't do it. Couldn't walk away from her and the baby. He didn't know what the hell that meant for his career or for him and Hannah. All he knew was that he couldn't leave.

"I'll take over the clinic while you recover from surgery."

"Hop in."

As soon as Alonso got into the cab and snapped his

belt on, Doc peeled away from the side of the road. "There's a cot in the back room you can sleep on, unless you plan to drive back to Hannah's ranch every night."

"I'll take the cot." He'd just as soon Hannah didn't know he'd changed his mind about Albuquerque. Not yet. Not until he had an answer for her when she asked why he'd stayed.

"I'll introduce you to my regular patients who come in once a week for blood-pressure checks and prescription refills. Then I'll fill you in on the house calls you'll have to make while I'm out."

"I don't have a vehicle."

"You can use Bertha."

"Pardon?"

Doc patted the dashboard. "This here is Bertha. She's a little rough around the edges, but she gets the job done. Fill her up at the convenience-store gas station and they'll charge it to my account. I'll let the sheriff know you'll be seeing my patients."

"Are you worried about the hip surgery?"

"I'm looking forward to the time off. Haven't had a vacation in years."

"Hell of a way to spend your vacation."

"I take what I can get."

"Are you sure your patients will see me?"

"Why wouldn't they?"

"They don't know me."

"You won't have any problems. Folks are grateful for my help."

"How do I handle payments?"

Doc waved a hand. "You'll figure it out soon enough."

When they reached town, Doc Snyder removed the

clinic key from his truck ring and offered it to Alonso. "Let yourself in. I'll see you in the morning."

Alonso was doing a good thing by remaining in Paradise to help Doc. But he knew from experience that it didn't matter how much good he did—in the end it wouldn't be enough.

Chapter Fourteen

A loud pounding woke Alonso and he checked his watch—eight thirty. The clinic opened at eight. He flew off the cot, shrugged into a fresh T-shirt and tugged on a pair of jeans, then shoved his feet into his hiking boots and hurried down the hall to the waiting room.

"Hold your horses!" He flipped the bolt, opened the door and came face-to-face with a chicken.

"Who are you?"

For a moment he thought the bird had spoken, then a head covered in gray wiry curls peeked around the chicken. "Where's Doc Snyder?"

Good question. "He should be here shortly. I'm Dr. Marquez."

"I've been waitin' outside in the cold for a half hour."

"I'm sorry." He opened the door wider. "Come in." She stepped past him and sat in a chair. He glanced between the woman and the bird, but both ignored him. He needed a shot of caffeine before he diagnosed the lady and her feathered friend. He returned to the storage room where he'd slept and studied his K-cup coffee choices stacked on the counter next to the Keurig machine. He picked a dark roast, waited two minutes, then, carrying his breakfast, he returned to the front room.

"I didn't get your name," he said.

She set the clucker on the floor. "Gertrude. Friends call me Gertie."

"What can I do for you, Gertie?"

"Doc switched my blood pressure medicine last week and said I had to come in today and have it checked."

"C'mon back."

She scooped the chicken off the floor.

"Leave your pet out here."

"Suit yourself." She followed him into an exam room and sat in the chair next to the door.

"Roll up your sweater sleeve, please."

After a minute she huffed. "How many times are you gonna take my blood pressure? Don't you know how to work that thing?"

Feisty old lady. "Your blood pressure is a little high, but not bad." He pressed two fingers against the dark blue vein on the inside of her wrist. "Pulse is fine." Then he felt her thyroid and lymph nodes. "I want to listen to your heart." When he was finished, he asked, "How old are you, Gertie?"

"Too old for you, young man."

He grinned.

"Eighty-one."

"Your eighty-one-year-old heartbeat is strong."

Her eyes twinkled. "Bob always told me I was too ornery to die."

"How old is Bob?"

"He's dead."

Jeez, his bedside manner needed work. He wasn't used to engaging patients in conversation—most of the time they were in shock or sedated. "I'm sorry to hear your husband passed away."

"Bob was my boyfriend."

He gaped at the old woman.

"My husband died thirty years ago of a heart attack. Fell off the tractor in the middle of the field. That man never missed a meal in his entire life, and when he was late for supper I knew he was gone."

Alonso was a surgeon, not a shrink. Hoping to avoid a therapy session with Gertie, he said, "Stay on your medication." He walked her back to the waiting room.

"Do I need to come in next week and have it checked again?"

"Sure." He noticed the droppings on the floor. "But leave your chicken at home."

"That's your chicken now." She opened the door.

"Hey, you can't leave the bird here."

"Doc and I have an agreement. He takes care of me and I pay him in chickens." She pointed to the clucker. "That there is a prize laying hen."

"Doc's having hip surgery and he won't be back for a few weeks."

"Then, keep the hen for yourself."

Alonso sipped his coffee and stared at his supper. Where the heck was Doc? The clinic phone rang. "Hello?"

"Alonso, I can't make it in today," Doc Snyder said. "I'm just getting home from a house call I went on after midnight. I'm in no shape to drive. Look behind the counter and you'll see a stack of files. Those patients are coming in today. I'll bring Bertha by later."

"But—"

The dial tone sounded in his ear. The chicken forgotten, he perused the files. There were ten people scheduled for the day. He was used to seeing three times that many. This job was going to be a breeze. He walked to the back of the clinic to make a second cup of coffee when the front door banged open and a voice called out. "Doc! Come quick!"

Alonso did an about-face and rushed back down the hallway. A middle-aged man stood in the doorway, holding a young boy with a bleeding head wound.

"He fell off his horse." The man's face was stark white and Alonso worried he'd faint if he didn't set the boy down soon.

"I'm Dr. Marquez. I'm filling in for Doc." He took the boy from the man's arms. "Follow me."

Alonso laid the boy on the table in the exam room, then checked his pupils. "Has he come to at all?"

"No."

The answer sent a cold chill down Alonso's back. "How long has he been unconscious?"

"About thirty minutes. I got here as fast as I could."

Alonso felt the boy's skull and neck, then checked his reflexes before probing the cut on his forehead. "How old is he?"

"Seven."

"Was he wearing a riding helmet?"

"No." The father's voice shook.

Alonso wanted to ask what the hell a seven-year-old was doing riding a horse without wearing the proper head gear, but the father's tormented expression told him the man was already blaming himself for his son's accident. "What's his name?"

"Billy. Billy Johnson. I'm his father, Earl."

Alonso's gut insisted the boy had a severe concussion or a possible brain bleed, but he needed a CT scan to confirm it. The clinic was limited to a single X-ray machine. He grasped Billy's hand. "If you can hear me, Billy, squeeze my hand." *Nothing.*

"Open your eyes, Billy."

The boy's eyes moved beneath his closed lids. The pressure in Alonso's chest intensified until it suffocated him. "Billy!"

The boy opened his eyes and stared unseeingly at Alonso.

"Looks as if he's going to be okay," the father said.

It was a good sign that Billy opened his eyes, but Alonso couldn't shake the feeling that the kid's injury was severe. "He needs a CT scan. If there's bleeding in the brain, he'll have to have surgery."

"Albuquerque and Gallup are about the same distance from here. Which hospital should I take him to?"

Billy might not have two hours. "He needs to be airlifted." Alonso left the room and made an emergency call to 911, requesting a life-flight helicopter. When he returned to the room, he said, "We're meeting the helicopter outside of town. We'll take your truck."

"I can't afford to pay for a helicopter." The man shoved his hands through his hair. "Billy woke up once." He glanced at his son, who lay motionless.

Alonso second-guessed himself. Was he panicking or had he made a rational, reasonable decision based on his exam and his experience treating trauma patients? "I'm not taking a chance with your son's life. This is more serious than a concussion." He started an IV in Billy's arm, then lifted him off the table. "Are you coming with me, or am I going alone with your son?"

The father led the way outside and Alonso laid Billy down in the backseat of Earl's truck. Earl started the engine and Alonso told him the location where the helicopter intended to set down. Fifteen minutes later Earl parked on the shoulder of the road next to the open field and they waited.

Alonso took Billy's pulse—the boy's breathing was shallow. He'd made the right decision to call 911. Billy's fall had been an accident and he might have hit his head even if he'd worn a riding helmet. He just hoped the kid would make it. His thoughts turned to Hannah and the child she carried. She'd insist that their son or daughter wear a helmet if they rode horses, but she might not be able to prevent an accident from happening. He imagined himself standing in Earl's shoes—it was bound to happen sooner or later because you couldn't protect those you cared about from all harm.

"Billy's been riding since he could sit a horse," Earl said. "Avalanche is almost twenty years old. You won't find a better-behaved horse. Billy was trotting him in the corral when Avalanche stumbled. It happened so fast."

Alonso felt bad for the father, but there was no time to reassure him as the helicopter came into sight.

"I've never been on a helicopter," Earl said.

"I was in the military. It's a breeze." Once the chopper landed, the crew carried a stretcher to the truck and Alonso helped them put Billy on it. While one of the medics strapped him down, Alonso informed them of the boy's condition and the need for a CT scan and possibly surgery to stop any hemorrhaging in the brain.

"Is the father coming?" the medic asked.

"I am." Earl handed his truck keys to Alonso. "Leave the truck at the clinic. I'll pick it up…whenever."

"Good luck." Alonso watched until the helicopter disappeared from sight, then drove back to the clinic, hoping his gut was wrong and the boy didn't have a brain bleed. As he approached town, a silver Civic heading in the opposite direction sped past him on the highway. *Luke*. Sooner or later, Hannah would find out he'd stayed in Paradise. He should tell her that he was taking over for Doc, but then she'd ask why, and to be honest he didn't know yet what his hanging around meant for their relationship.

When he arrived at the clinic, there were several vehicles parked out front, including Bertha. It was about time Doc showed up to help him out. The waiting room looked more like a flea market than a medical office. One woman held a handmade quilt on her lap. Another lady had a plastic cake container. The only man in the room sat with a burlap bag marked "popcorn seed." And Gertrude's damned chicken was waddling all over the place clucking its head off.

"Is Doc Snyder here?" Alonso asked the group.

"He left a few minutes ago."

Great. "Sorry about the wait. There was an emergency this morning."

"Who?" the woman with the cake asked.

"Billy Johnson fell off a horse and hit his head."

"Is he going to be okay?" the older man asked.

If Alonso said he didn't know, then his patients wouldn't have much confidence in his doctoring ability. But if he said yes and Billy took a turn for the worse, they wouldn't trust him. Either way he couldn't win. "Billy needed a CT scan and Doc doesn't have a machine at the clinic, so a life-flight helicopter is flying him to Albuquerque."

The group grew quiet—they knew without being told that Billy's condition was serious. "I'm Dr. Marquez."

"We know. Doc said you were taking over until he recovered from his surgery." The lady with the quilt on her lap spoke. She wore a pinched look on her face and appeared to be in pain.

"What's your name?" Alonso asked.

"Maryellen Trumpet."

He searched through the files but didn't see a Maryellen. "I can't find your paperwork," he said.

"I wasn't supposed to visit Doc until late next week, but..." She set the quilt on the chair next to her, revealing her big belly. "I think the baby's coming now."

Alonso stared in shock. "When's your due date?"

"Three days ago."

"Why haven't you gone to the hospital in Cañon City?"

"I'm using a midwife, but she came down with the flu this week and she told me to go ahead and let Doc handle the delivery."

Alonso felt a moment of panic. He'd never delivered a baby before. "Is there a backup midwife you can call?"

"It's too late," she said.

"What do you mean, too late?"

"My water broke earlier this morning. The pains are two minutes apart now." As if on cue, Maryellen groaned when a contraction hit her.

"You gonna just stand there, Doc, or help this poor woman?" the man next to her spoke.

"I'm going to help her," Alonso said. As if he had a choice.

"Hey, Hannah, I thought Alonso was going back to Albuquerque?"

As soon as Rambo heard Luke's voice he bolted

past Hannah in Buster's stall and raced toward his best friend. She set aside the rake she'd been using to muck the stall. "He did go back. Why?"

"I passed a pickup on the road and it looked like Alonso behind the wheel."

Hannah's heart pounded inside her chest. "You must be mistaken."

"Maybe, but it sure looked like him."

Hannah shoved the pitchfork at him. "You and Rambo finish up." She left the barn and jogged to the house. Once inside she pulled her cell phone from her pocket and dialed Doc's home phone. His wife, Marlene, answered.

"Marlene, this is Hannah Buck."

"Hello, dear. How are you?"

"I'm fine. Is Doc at the clinic right now?"

"Didn't you hear?"

"Hear what?"

"He's taking time off to have that hip replacement done. We're driving to Albuquerque tomorrow."

"Who's running the clinic?"

"Alonso Marquez agreed to see Ed's patients."

Her brother hadn't seen a ghost.

"By the way, how's Luke doing?"

"He's doing much better, thanks for asking."

"I'm glad. Ed's sleeping, but I can wake him up if you need to speak with him right away."

"It's not important. Tell him that I'm thinking of him and wishing him a speedy recovery."

"You and me both. That man gets cranky when he has to sit still for more than a half hour."

"Take care, Marlene." Hannah ended the call and stared into space. What did this mean?

The back door crashed open and Luke walked inside, dragging Rambo behind him. The dog had sunk his teeth into the bottom of Luke's pant leg and wouldn't let go.

"You need to train Rambo to stop doing that. I can't have an ankle biter around when the baby starts crawling." As soon as the words left her mouth, Hannah sucked in a quick breath.

Luke stared at her bug-eyed. "What baby?"

This wasn't how she'd planned to break the news to her brother. "You're going to be an uncle." She forced a smile.

"Whose baby is it? Alonso or Seth?"

She scowled. "I broke up with Seth two years ago."

"Girls sleep with their old boyfriends all the time."

How would he know that? "Alonso is the father."

"I know you get pissed off at me because you say I'm immature and I need to grow up, but I'd never desert a girl if I got her pregnant."

"Alonso didn't desert me."

"Then, why did he say he was going back to Albuquerque?"

"Things are complicated." At her brother's scowl, she added, "But Alonso is taking full responsibility for this baby."

"He doesn't want to be a father."

"It's not that simple, Luke."

Her brother pulled out a chair and sat down at the table. "I'm almost seventeen. I can handle the truth."

"If I knew the truth then I'd share it with you. I don't exactly know why Alonso wants nothing to do with raising our baby."

"Why don't you ask him?"

"What good would it do? We raise bison and Alonso is a trauma surgeon. Our lives are going in different directions."

"Did you ask him to stay?"

She dropped her gaze.

"Are you afraid he'll say no?"

"Maybe. I think I'd rather raise this baby on my own than wake up each morning knowing I guilted Alonso into staying here when he doesn't love me."

"Did he say he didn't love you?"

"He never said he did or didn't."

"Do you love him?"

She felt like a punching bag—each of her brother's questions knocking the air out of her. "Yes, I love him." She sighed. "And you weren't wrong about thinking you saw Alonso earlier. He's filling in at the clinic while Doc has surgery."

"Then, you have time to convince him to stay." When Hannah remained silent, Luke asked, "You gotta tell him that you love him."

"What if it doesn't make a difference?"

"You had your heart broken before. What's the big deal?"

That was the problem—she hadn't been in love with Seth—not the way she'd fallen for Alonso.

ALONSO DIDN'T THINK his day could get any crazier as he helped Maryellen onto the exam table. He offered a smile, hoping to reassure the expectant mother. And maybe himself, too.

"I called the midwife again and told her Doc Snyder wasn't around. She'll get here as soon as she can," Maryellen said.

"Good." Maybe he wouldn't have to deliver the baby.

"Is anyone else coming to be with you?"

"My husband's on his way from North Dakota. He works in the oil fields up there." Maryellen sucked in a breath when another contraction hit her.

He held her hand, all the while thinking of Hannah. Was this how she'd end up giving birth to their child—alone in Doc's clinic? When the contraction passed, he took her blood pressure. "Do you know what you're having?"

"A girl. We're naming her Caroline after my mother."

Alonso's memory raced through the pages of his medical textbooks, trying to recall the chapters on childbirth as he washed his hands and put on a paper gown.

Maryellen groaned loudly and he said, "Practice your breathing." He had no idea what the hell he was talking about and was glad Maryellen wasn't panicking. He opened a cupboard and found several clean towels. A knock on the door caught him by surprise. "Maybe that's the midwife." He opened the door and found Hannah standing in the hallway, looking more beautiful than she had a right to be.

"You didn't leave. Why?" she asked.

For a million and one reasons. Did she want to know them all? Right now?

He glanced at Maryellen, who appeared more interested in his and Hannah's conversation than her labor pains.

"Is it because of the baby?" Hannah asked.

"That, but…mostly it was you," he said.

Hannah smiled.

"Doc," Maryellen said. "I need to push."

"Oh, my God." Hannah stepped into the room. "You're having a baby."

"I'm trying," Maryellen said.

"Have you ever delivered a baby, Alonso?" Hannah asked.

"No."

Maryellen's eyes rounded.

"It's okay," Hannah said, taking the woman's hand in hers. "I've delivered calves before. I can help."

Alonso's patient didn't look reassured. "I'm having a baby, not a calf."

"I'm Hannah."

"Maryellen."

"Nice to meet you, Maryellen. How close are the contractions?"

"About a minute apart."

Hannah looked at Alonso and the confidence in him that shone in her eyes spurred him into action. "Help Maryellen out of her dress and put this sheet over her." Alonso turned his back while Hannah helped undress Maryellen. He found a scissors and thread to tie off the umbilical cord and a suction bulb in case he needed to clear the baby's airway.

"Can I push now?" Maryellen grimaced.

Alonso looked between her legs and saw that the baby's head was crowning. No turning back now. "Slow and easy," he said.

Sweat broke out across his brow as the baby's head came farther out with Maryellen's next push. "Does your husband have hair?" Alonso asked, hoping to distract the mother from the pain she was in.

"No," she gasped. "He shaves his head. Why?"

"Your baby girl is bald, too."

Maryellen laughed, then squeezed Hannah's hand when another contraction hit.

After three pushes, the baby slid into Alonso's hands, and he placed the crying infant on Maryellen's chest. After he tied off and cut the cord, he briskly rubbed the little body and a loud cry escaped her tiny mouth. "Her lungs are working."

"You did it, Maryellen." Hannah smiled at the mother and daughter.

A few minutes later, Alonso delivered the placenta and Hannah helped Maryellen clean up while Alonso weighed the baby. "Seven pounds eleven ounces." He wrapped the little girl in a towel, then listened to her chest. "Caroline's heart and lungs sound fine." He handed the baby to Maryellen just as the exam door burst open, knocking Hannah into Alonso's chest.

A wild-eyed bald man shouted, "Where's Maryellen?"

"I'm right here."

Alonso pulled Hannah aside so the father could see his wife and newborn daughter. He kissed Maryellen, then the baby. "She's as beautiful as you, honey."

Alonso and Hannah left the room, giving the new parents time alone.

"You were wonderful in there." Alonso brushed his fingers across his cheek. He stared into Hannah's baby blues. "I can't go back to Albuquerque."

"Why not?"

"I love you."

Tears spilled down her cheeks.

His heart thudded painfully in his chest. How had he ever believed leaving Hannah was the right thing to do? "I love you and our baby, but loving you both scares me to death."

"Parenthood can be frightening, but we'll help each other through it."

He shook his head. "It's so damned risky, Hannah. What if something happens to the baby?" *Or you.*

"There are no guarantees in life. We do the best we can, make the best decisions we can and hope in the end everything works out." She went up on tiptoe and kissed his mouth.

He wasn't sure it was as simple as Hannah made it seem, but he didn't want to go back to the ER and get swallowed up by all the darkness again. Hannah had shown him there was still beauty and goodness left in the world—all he had to do was give her his hand and she and the baby would keep him looking forward to a future filled with love and hope, not hate and destruction.

"I've been doing a lot of thinking, and I'd like to try working at the clinic with Doc when he returns from his hip-replacement surgery."

"But you can help more people in a hospital."

"I've had my fill of trauma surgeries."

"Are you sure this town, the ranch, me…are enough for you?"

"More than sure." He threaded his fingers through hers. "I need you, Hannah. I need your strength. Your courage." He sucked in a deep breath and released it slowly. "I love you for wanting to bring my child into the world, knowing that you might have had to do it on your own."

Hannah wrapped her arms around Alonso and hugged

him. "And I love you for being brave enough to give you, me and the baby a chance to be a real family."

He stared into her eyes. "You have my word that I'll be by your side every step of the way no matter what life throws at us."

"I don't need your word. I just need your heart."

When Alonso kissed her, Hannah felt a surge of joy rush through her body. The future suddenly looked brighter than she'd ever dreamed possible. Someone cleared their throat and Hannah broke off the kiss.

"Are you going to be much longer, Dr. Marquez? There's a lady in the waiting room who needs her insulin shot."

"Be right there." He smiled at Hannah. "Looks as if it'll be a long day."

"Will I see you later?"

He nodded. "I'm coming home tonight." Hannah and the baby were home now. Once Hannah left, he entered the waiting room and discovered every chair filled. Baked goods and casseroles were piling up on the counter. "Okay, who needs their insulin shot?"

"Me. I'm Gladys. I can't get the hang of that newfangled meter. It's always telling me my blood sugar is low, but I don't think it is."

Alonso checked Gladys's blood sugar, gave her the insulin shot and sent her on the way. Next, he stitched up Kevin Heppner's finger, which he'd gashed when he'd accidentally grabbed hold of a barbed-wire fence without a glove. Then he clipped and filed Mr. Livingston's toenails and recommended he get a pedicure every two months. The man argued that pedicures were for women, which ignited a discussion in the waiting area about the term *metrosexual*, after which Mr. Livingston loudly denied that he was gay.

Not long after Mr. Livingston left, the midwife arrived with two of her children in tow. The kids played with the chicken while their mother tended to Maryellen. Soon after, the new parents left with their baby.

The day slipped by and finally at six thirty he locked the front door. Exhausted, he stared at the messy waiting room. He stored the perishable food in the fridge—he wouldn't have to make his lunch for a month. Just when he was ready to turn out the lights he heard a scuffling sound—the chicken stared at him from the end of the hallway. "Where have you been all day?"

The bird waddled up to Alonso, then sat on top of his boots. "Make yourself comfortable, why don't you?"

He scooped up his new feathered friend. "I hope Rambo takes a liking to you." He got into Doc's truck and made a phone call on the way out of town.

"This is Dr. Marquez. A patient of mine was life-flighted to the hospital today and I'm calling to check on him."

"What's the patient's name?"

"Billy Johnson. Head-trauma victim."

"He went into surgery to stop a brain bleed shortly after he arrived. He's still in recovery."

"What's his prognosis?"

"Excellent. Dr. McNamara performed the operation."

Dr. McNamara was a well-respected surgeon. Billy had been in good hands. "Thanks for the update."

After a few miles Alonso glanced across the seat—his copilot had fallen asleep. It was almost eight o'clock when he pulled into the ranch yard. Rambo barked, and a moment later Hannah walked into the kitchen, Luke on her heels holding the puppy.

"Is everything okay?" she asked.

"Sorry I'm so late. The patients left me with a mess in the waiting room." He smiled. "It was a long day but a good day."

"Hannah said you're not going back to Albuquerque."

"I need to talk to you about that, Luke."

The teen glanced between the adults. "Okay."

"I'd like to marry your sister and I was hoping you'd approve."

"What about your job at the hospital?" Luke asked.

"I'm ready to move on to something different. A slower pace." Although today had been anything but slow.

Luke grinned. "Does marrying my sister mean you're going to live here on the ranch with her?"

"Yes."

"Then, heck yeah, you can marry my sister."

Hannah playfully punched Luke in the arm. "I'm seriously going to be outnumbered by males." She placed her hand over her stomach. "Let's hope we're having a girl."

"I want a boy." Luke set Rambo on the floor and the dog raced over to the door. "He's got to go outside."

Alone in the kitchen with Hannah, Alonso pulled her close for a hug. "Are you sure?" Hannah had had several hours to think about marrying him after she'd left the clinic. If she was having second thoughts, he wanted to know now.

"I'm more sure of you than anything else in my life."

"I'll work hard so you never lose faith in me." He kissed her gently, pledging his love to her.

"Hey, did you know there's a chicken out here?" Luke called through the screen door.

Alonso chuckled. "I guess it's a good thing we live on a ranch. Who knows what I'll be bringing home every night."

"I don't care how many critters you bring home as long as you're the one bringing them." Hannah pressed her mouth against his and Alonso tasted all that was good and beautiful—a future together, a family and a forever love.

Epilogue

"I knew Hannah would get her way." Luke walked into his bedroom, grinning.

Alonso shrugged into his suit jacket. "I underestimated your sister." Alonso had believed he'd have a few months to get used to the idea of becoming a married man but Hannah hadn't been willing to compromise on a wedding date.

"You sure you want to marry her? She can be bossy."

"Your sister's not bossy," he said. "She's persuasive." *And a seductress.* But Alonso couldn't very well admit to his soon-to-be brother-in-law that he hadn't put up much of a fight when Hannah had launched her campaign to move up the wedding date using her wiles in bed against him.

Only two weeks had passed since he'd taken over the clinic for Doc, but he'd settled into a routine with his patients that felt comfortable and right. And each night he came home to Hannah—the best part of his day. Later in bed, after they made love, he'd rest his hand on her tummy and imagine what their child would be like. What its personality would be.

Some nights Alonso swore it was as if the baby was communicating with him. His palm would heat up against Hannah's belly and the warm sensation would then travel up his arm, into his chest and straight to his heart, bringing him a sense of peace he'd never felt before.

He turned away from the mirror. "Yes, I'm sure I want to marry your sister."

"Cool. I'm glad she won't be all alone after I graduate from high school."

"Don't worry about your sister. I'll take good care of her and your niece or nephew. You just make sure you graduate."

"I will. I promise."

"Is it warming up outside?" Alonso asked.

"No, but the sun is out."

Hannah had enlisted Maria Fitzgerald's help in planning the ceremony at the Blue Bison. Cruz's father-in-law, José, had prepared the food for the guests and Betsy from the Red Bluff Diner had baked the wedding cake. Michael came up the weekend before the wedding and helped Luke build a maze out of hay bales for the kids and Rambo to play in after the ceremony.

"Doc Snyder wants to talk to you before you go outside," Luke said.

"Sure, send him in."

A minute later Doc entered Luke's bedroom and shut the door.

"Hey, Doc."

"Alonso." Doc held out a brand-new black Stetson. "What's this for?"

"For taking care of my practice while I recuperated."

Doc Snyder had recovered quickly from his hip-replacement surgery and was scheduled to return to work in another week. Alonso wasn't sure what he was going to do about a job, but Hannah didn't seem worried, so he'd taken his cue from her and decided that things would work out the way they were meant to be. "You didn't have to buy me a hat." Alonso examined the Stetson. It wasn't his first cowboy hat but it was his first nice one. He tried it on, surprised it fit well.

"Now you look like a country doctor."

"I guess I do." Alonso stared at his image in the mirror. There was no trace of the soldier that had followed him home from Afghanistan. That part of his life was over now. He'd hold the good memories close—his friendships with his comrades—then let the bad ones go.

"I have a proposition for you," Doc said.

"What's that?"

"I've decided to retire and I want you to take over my practice."

Shocked, Alonso didn't know what to say.

"I've been meaning to retire for a while now, but I didn't want to turn my patients over to just anyone."

"You still have some gas left in you, Doc." He expected a smile or a chuckle but the older man's expression remained sober. "You're serious, aren't you?"

"I'm not getting any younger, and now that I can walk pain-free, Marlene wants to travel. We've never been to Italy, where her great-grandparents are from. We just bought our plane tickets. We're leaving in March."

"But—"

"I don't mind consulting on cases if you need a second opinion, but I'm not coming into the clinic every day." He cleared his throat. "Being a country doctor might not be challenging enough for a man with your talents, but folks like you." He straightened his shoulders. "You think you could be happy taking care of your friends and neighbors instead of strangers?"

Taking care of friends and neighbors... Not bodies without names whom he never saw again after they left the surgery suite. Doc was offering Alonso the opportunity to serve people who would become part of his life. "Are you sure you're ready to hang up your stethoscope?"

"Positive. If I bring home any more chickens, Marlene will pluck me for dinner."

Alonso chuckled. "I'd be honored to take over your practice."

"You won't make as much money as surgeons in Albuquerque."

"Money's overrated."

"You won't think so when you have more kids."

"Whoa, let me get used to having one first."

The doctor offered his hand. "I don't know what brought you to Paradise, Alonso, but I do know you're the best thing that's happened to Hannah and Luke. God knows that girl deserves some happiness in her life. You do right by her and my patients, and I'll be forever in your debt."

Alonso patted Doc on the shoulder. "I'm ready to see my bride." He followed Doc outside to the front porch, where the ceremony would take place. Hannah had insisted on no bridesmaids or groomsmen. Luke was giving Hannah away and the rest of the onlookers had gathered in the front yard.

Alonso had invited his sisters and his mother, and they'd been thrilled for him and Hannah. His mother had been especially excited about another grandchild and had offered to take care of the baby anytime Hannah and Alonso wanted to get away together. He smiled at his mother, who stood by the porch steps, tears of happiness in her eyes.

He hadn't counted on being this nervous before the ceremony, but his knees felt as if they were held together with rubber bands. He searched the crowd and spotted Riley and Cruz. They came forward and joined him on the porch.

"This is a big step," Riley said. "You ready?"

"I thought I was." He looked at Cruz. "I'm afraid I'll screw this up."

"Welcome to my world." Cruz smiled, then winced when Riley elbowed him in the ribs.

"You two haven't had it easy all these years, there's no question about that. But you both beat the odds and found a better life outside of the barrio. Let yourselves believe that you deserve to be happy."

"Easy for the rich guy to say," Alonso said.

Riley fought a grin. "I hope I wasn't just a wallet to you two."

Alonso and Cruz exchanged glances, then Alonso said, "You've been the big brother we always wished we'd had."

"And the father we never had," Cruz said.

"And a mentor we probably didn't deserve," Alonso added.

Cruz cleared his throat. "Not a day goes by that we don't appreciate what you've done for us."

"That's enough of the sentimental crap." Riley clasped both men by the shoulders. "I'm proud of you guys."

Someone turned on the music and the bridal march began to play. Riley and Cruz returned to the lawn and stood by their wives and children. The minister opened the front door and Luke escorted the bride outside.

Hannah was breathtaking in a simple white wedding dress. She carried a bouquet of red roses, and a dark red ribbon held her hair back from her face. The minister asked who gave the bride away, but Alonso didn't hear a word after that as he lost himself in the love for him shining in Hannah's eyes.

* * * * *

Be sure to look for Marin Thomas's next book in her COWBOYS OF THE RIO GRANDE *series,* *available in 2016* *wherever Harlequin books are sold!*

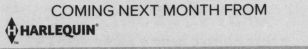
#1573 TEXAS REBELS: QUINCY
Texas Rebels • by Linda Warren

Jenny Walker was his brother's high school sweetheart...and therefore off-limits to Quincy Rebel. But the time has come to admit his feelings to her. Will Quincy risk family loyalty for the woman he loves?

#1574 HER MISTLETOE COWBOY
Forever, Texas • by Marie Ferrarella

When journalist Kimberly Lee is injured while working on a story on The Healing Ranch, Garrett White Eagle takes her in. But the rancher and the writer soon find that wounds old and new might just heal in time for Christmas...

#1575 THE LAWMAN'S CHRISTMAS PROPOSAL
The Hitching Post Hotel • by Barbara White Daille

Big-city cop Mitch Weston and single mom Andi Price reluctantly agree to a pretend engagement for the holidays. But when the time comes to "break up," Andi discovers she wants the fake relationship to be real.

#1576 A CHRISTMAS WEDDING FOR THE COWBOY
by Mary Leo

When bronc rider Carson Grant gets dumped by his fiancée only weeks before his Christmas nuptials, wedding planner Zoe Smart is happy to step in—as the bride! But is their relationship jinxed from the start?

REQUEST YOUR FREE BOOKS!
2 FREE NOVELS PLUS 2 FREE GIFTS!

HARLEQUIN®

American Romance®

LOVE, HOME & HAPPINESS

YES! Please send me 2 FREE Harlequin® American Romance® novels and my 2 FREE gifts (gifts are worth about $10). After receiving them, if I don't wish to receive any more books, I can return the shipping statement marked "cancel." If I don't cancel, I will receive 4 brand-new novels every month and be billed just $4.74 per book in the U.S. or $5.49 per book in Canada. That's a savings of at least 12% off the cover price! It's quite a bargain! Shipping and handling is just 50¢ per book in the U.S. and 75¢ per book in Canada.* I understand that accepting the 2 free books and gifts places me under no obligation to buy anything. I can always return a shipment and cancel at any time. Even if I never buy another book, the two free books and gifts are mine to keep forever.

154/354 HDN GHZZ

Name	(PLEASE PRINT)	

Address		Apt. #

City	State/Prov.	Zip/Postal Code

Signature (if under 18, a parent or guardian must sign)

Mail to the **Reader Service:**
IN U.S.A.: P.O. Box 1867, Buffalo, NY 14240-1867
IN CANADA: P.O. Box 609, Fort Erie, Ontario L2A 5X3

Want to try two free books from another line?
Call 1-800-873-8635 or visit www.ReaderService.com.

* Terms and prices subject to change without notice. Prices do not include applicable taxes. Sales tax applicable in N.Y. Canadian residents will be charged applicable taxes. Offer not valid in Quebec. This offer is limited to one order per household. Not valid for current subscribers to Harlequin American Romance books. All orders subject to credit approval. Credit or debit balances in a customer's account(s) may be offset by any other outstanding balance owed by or to the customer. Please allow 4 to 6 weeks for delivery. Offer available while quantities last.

Your Privacy—The Reader Service is committed to protecting your privacy. Our Privacy Policy is available online at www.ReaderService.com or upon request from the Reader Service.

We make a portion of our mailing list available to reputable third parties that offer products we believe may interest you. If you prefer that we not exchange your name with third parties, or if you wish to clarify or modify your communication preferences, please visit us at www.ReaderService.com/consumerschoice or write to us at Reader Service Preference Service, P.O. Box 9062, Buffalo, NY 14240-9062. Include your complete name and address.

SPECIAL EXCERPT FROM

HARLEQUIN®

American Romance®

*When journalist Kim Lee is injured on the job in
Forever, Texas, she is unwillingly taken in by cowboy
Garrett White Eagle. The journalist never believed
in love, but Santa might just write her and the rugged
rancher a happy ending this Christmas!*

*Read on for a sneak preview of
HER MISTLETOE COWBOY, the latest volume
in the FOREVER, TEXAS miniseries.*

"Well, Garrett-the-other-White-Eagle, you have no cell
reception out here," Kim complained. As if to prove her
point, she held up the phone that still wasn't registering
a signal.

Garrett nodded. "It's been known to happen on
occasion," he acknowledged.

She was right. This was a hellhole. "How long an
occasion?" she wanted to know.

The shrug was quick and generally indifferent, as
if there were far more important matters to tend to. "It
varies." He nodded at her compact. "What's wrong with
your car?"

She glanced over her shoulder, as if to check that it was
still where it was supposed to be. "Nothing, I just didn't
want to drive it if I didn't know where I was going." A
small pout accompanied the next accusation. "I lost the
GPS signal."

Garrett took that in stride. Nothing, he supposed,
unusual about that either, even though neither he nor

anyone he knew even had a GPS in their car. They relied far more on their own instincts and general familiarity with the area.

He did move just a little closer now. He saw that she was watching him, as if uncertain whether or not to trust him yet. He could see her side of it. After all, it was just the two of them out here and she only had his word for who he was.

"You can follow me, then," he told her, then added a smile that was intended to dazzle her—several of Miss Joan's waitresses had told him his smile was one of his best features. "Consider me your guiding light."

You're cute, no doubt about that, but I'll hold off on the guiding light part, if you don't mind, Kim thought. She stifled a sigh as she got in behind the wheel of her car. She *knew* she should have dug in and fought getting stuck with this assignment.

Don't miss
HER MISTLETOE COWBOY
by USA TODAY *bestselling author Marie Ferrarella,*
available December 2015 wherever
Harlequin® American Romance®
books and ebooks are sold.

www.Harlequin.com

Love the Harlequin book
you just read?

Your opinion matters.

Review this book on your favorite
book site, review site, blog or your own
social media properties and share
your opinion with other readers!

THE WORLD IS BETTER WITH

Romance

Harlequin has everything from contemporary, passionate and heartwarming to suspenseful and inspirational stories.

Whatever your mood, we have a romance just for you!

Connect with us to find your next great read, special offers and more.

f /HarlequinBooks

🐦 @HarlequinBooks

www.HarlequinBlog.com

www.Harlequin.com/Newsletters

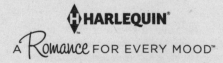

◈ HARLEQUIN®

A *Romance* FOR EVERY MOOD™

www.Harlequin.com